Kylie Jean

by Marci Peschke

illustrated by Tuesday Mourning

PICTURE WINDOW BOOKS
a capstone imprint

Kylie Jean is published by Picture Window Books
A Capstone Imprint
1710 Roe Crest Drive
North Mankato, Minnesota 56003
www.capstonepub.com

Previously published as three separate library-bound volumes:
Blueberry Queen 978-1-4048-6756-7
Drama Queen 978-1-4048-6757-4
Singing Queen 978-1-4048-6800-7

Library of Congress Cataloging-in-Publication Data is available at the Library of
Congress website.

Design Element Credit:
Shutterstock/blue67design

Printed in China.
009285

Kylie Jean

All About Me, Kylie Jean!

My name is Kylie Jean Carter. I live in a big, sunny, yellow house on Peachtree Lane in Jacksonville, Texas with Momma, Daddy, and my two brothers, T.J. and Ugly Brother.

T.J. is my older brother, and Ugly Brother is . . . well . . . he's really a dog. Don't you go telling him he is a dog. Okay? I mean it. He thinks he is a real true person.

He is a black-and-white bulldog. His front looks like his back, all smashed in. His face is all droopy like he's sad, but he's not.

His two front teeth stick out and his tongue hangs down. (Now you know why his name is Ugly Brother.)

Everyone I love to the moon and back lives in Jacksonville. Nanny, Pa, Granny, Pappy, my aunts, my uncles, and my cousins all live here. I'm extra lucky, because I can see all of them any time I want to!

My momma says I'm pretty. She says I have eyes as blue as the summer sky and a smile as sweet as an angel. (Momma says pretty is as pretty does. That means being nice to the old folks, taking care of little animals, and respecting my momma and daddy.)

But I'm pretty on the outside and on the inside. My hair is long, brown, and curly.

I wear it in a ponytail sometimes, but my absolute most favorite is when Momma pulls it back in a princess style on special days.

I just gave you a little hint about my big dream. Ever since I was a bitty baby I have wanted to be an honest-to-goodness beauty queen. I even know the wave. It's side to side, nice and slow, with a dazzling smile. I practice all the time, because everybody knows beauty queens need to have a perfect wave.

I'm Kylie Jean, and I'm going to be a beauty queen. Just you wait and see!

Blueberry Queen

Table of Contents

Chapter One
Going to the Farm

The sun is so hot today! My can of orange soda started getting warm as soon as I walked out of the Drive-N-Go with Momma. We're going to the farm to help Nanny and Pa pick blueberries in the blueberry patch. My cousin Lucy will be there too. She and I like to pick a few and eat a few.

We climb back in the van and the heat sucks all the air outta me like a popped balloon, so I sip my orange soda long and slow.

Momma is busy driving, but I'm busy thinking about being a beauty queen.

My brother T.J. says they don't let little girls be beauty queens, but T.J. is only right half the time. That means I have a chance. Ugly Brother doesn't say much about it. He usually doesn't say much about anything.

Before long, Momma turns on Lickskillet Road, and we can see the farm. Nanny and Pa have a red house and a red barn. They have horses, a huge garden, and a pond. It is magnificent!

Pa is standing in the blueberry patch. He shouts, "Where y'all been? I've been workin' since the rooster crowed."

"Oh Daddy, you know I have things to do at home, too," Momma tells Pa, smiling at him as we climb out of the car. "I've been tryin' out my new recipes for the Blueberry Bake-Off."

She laughs and adds, "Don't you go worrying now, Pa, I won't make you wait two weeks for the Blueberry Festival to try it. I brought you a piece."

My cousin Lucy runs over. "Let's go play!" she says. Then she reaches for my orange soda. "Come on, Kylie Jean!" she shouts. "Just one sip! Pleeease." But I frown and pull it away from her.

Momma turns. She says, "Kylie Jean, you share that soda with your cousin. Pretty is as pretty does." Momma has her arms crossed. That's how I know she means business.

I crinkle up my face a little, but I give Lucy a sip of my orange soda. Then we smile and head over to sit in the shade of a big tree.

Pretty soon, Pa calls us over to the big green tractor. He asks, "Who wants the first ride?"

Lucy and I look at each other. She knows I want the first ride. "Kylie Jean, since you gave me a sip of your orange soda, I want you to take the first turn," Lucy says sweetly. Then we hug.

I climb up on the tractor and sit in front of Pa on the big seat. The tractor starts up, and it's loud, like T.J.'s lawnmower gone crazy. Pa begins to drive out to the pond, and I wave just like a real beauty queen. The tractor is loud, but I pretend I'm in a parade.

The pond is deep, blue, and perfectly round. Just like the blueberries in the blueberry patch.

Suddenly an idea strikes my brain just like lightning. I could be the Blueberry Festival Queen!

The rest of the day, I spend my time picking blueberries and dreaming about being a beauty queen.

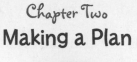

Chapter Two
Making a Plan

I need a plan if I'm going to be the Blueberry Queen.

One thing I know for sure about making a plan is that you need another person. Pa always says that two heads are better than one.

So on Saturday morning, I wake up real bright and early. Before I go downstairs to eat my blueberry pancakes, I start working on my plan.

First things first, I try to think of a person to help me.

The first person I think of is my cousin Lucy. The problem is, Lucy's just a kid, like me. She won't be able to help me. Plus, she's kind of shy, and I need someone brave.

But Lucy has a big sister, Lilly. Lilly is good at figuring things out, so I give her a call on her cell phone.

She says, "Hey, Kylie Jean, what's up? I'm at cheerleading practice. Is everything okay?"

"I need help with a special beauty queen project," I tell her. "Can you help me?"

Lilly laughs. "Oh, aren't you somethin'? Are you still stuck on being a beauty queen?" she asks.

I'm not so sure that's funny. I wait a second, and then ask, "Are you still stuck on being a cheerleader?"

For a second, she gets kinda quiet. Then she says, "Okay, I see your point. When can I come over?"

"How about now?" I say.

Lilly laughs. "I'm busy right now, sugar," she whispers. I hear a whistle blow. "I'll be at your house at 2," Lilly says. Then she hangs up.

I already have a partner, and I didn't even eat breakfast yet! My plan is going just perfectly.

After I eat my cereal, I spend the morning helping our neighbor, Miss Clarabelle, weed her flowerbeds.

It's a good thing it ain't too hot yet, since weeding can be hard work. I think I could wilt just like one of those flowers.

Miss Clarabelle and I sit on the ground and look real careful. Finding weeds is like finding a bug in a rug. She's wearing a really big purple hat and purple gardening gloves. Purple is her color.

I'm wearing my pink tennis shoes and a pair of gloves with pink bows. You guessed it! Pink is my color.

After pulling so many weeds, I'm covered with dirt. I tell Miss Clarabelle that I have a special meeting today, and I have to quit working. "But I'll come back soon and help you out again," I add.

Miss Clarabelle never stops pulling the weeds. She just says, "You run on, sugar. You've been a lot of help to me today."

I wave to her purple hat and run home across the yard, careful not to step in the flowers. Miss Clarabelle would say a crushed flower is a powerful sad thing.

I take a bath and put on a fancy dress. I want to look my best. When Lilly sees me looking so pretty, she'll know I mean business.

Once I'm ready, I sit quietly in our fancy living room, which is right next to the front door. That's where I'll wait for my cousin.

I sit on the sofa, waiting for Lilly. I hear Momma's tall clock *tick . . . tock . . . tick . . . tock.* Then I cross my arms just like Momma does when she's waiting for something and it's taking too long.

After a hundred years, the front door opens.

Lilly shouts, "Hey y'all, anyone here? Kylie Jean?" She doesn't see me waiting in the living room.

I don't shout back. Momma says shouting is not ladylike, and right now I'm trying my hardest to be a beauty queen. So instead of yelling, I gracefully hop off the sofa and walk over to the front door.

When I tap her on the back, Lilly lets out a scream! Then she spins around and says, "Kylie Jean, you scared the life outta me!"

When we're done laughing, Lilly looks me over, top to toe. I cross my arms again and smile as she notices my pretty dress.

Lilly nods. "I see that you're serious about this," she says.

"I am," I say. I grab her hand and ask, "What do we do first?"

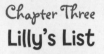

Chapter Three
Lilly's List

"Let's use T.J.'s computer," Lilly says.

I know that's a bad idea. Before I can stop myself, I snort. I put my hand over my mouth. Beauty queens do not snort!

"What's so funny?" Lilly asks.

"You can use the computer if you can stand the smell in T.J.'s room," I say. "Momma says it stinks worse than the pigsty down at Pa's farm."

Lilly makes a face and pulls her shirt up over her nose. Her eyes are laughing.

She says, "Okay, let's do this."

We push open the door and climb over T.J.'s dirty clothes, sports stuff, and smelly shoes. They cover the floor. I wave at T.J.'s sleeping hamster in its cage.

His computer screen is black. Lilly jiggles the mouse and the screen lights up with a picture of the Dallas Cowboys. Lilly goes on the Internet and types some stuff. Then she prints something out.

"This is the form you need to fill out to sign up for the pageant," Lilly tells me. She sees me looking confused and adds, "The pageant is the beauty queen competition."

"Right," I say. "I know that." Lilly winks.

We go back to the fancy living room.

"First things first," Lilly says, sounding just like Momma when she says it. "We need to make a list."

"What about that form?" I ask.

Lilly waves her hand. "We can fill that out later," she tells me. She points at the paper. "There's some other stuff you're gonna need first."

I lean over to look at the paper.

Lilly glances at me. Then she reads aloud, "All applicants for the Blueberry Queen must have the following: a sponsor, an entry fee of twenty-five dollars, a recent photo, posters, a recommendation letter, a three-hundred-word essay, and their own transportation."

My mouth drops open.

"Are you serious?" I whisper.

Twenty-five dollars? Where am I supposed to get that? And I don't even know what the rest of that stuff is. Being a beauty queen sounds way harder than I thought!

Lilly sits back on the sofa and stares at me. "Well, that's quite a list, Kylie Jean," she says. She puts her hand under her chin. I'm waiting for her to say something. All of a sudden, she looks at her watch. "Oh, I gotta run. I'll help you out another time, okay?"

"What about the form?" I ask her. I'm feeling nervous. This is an awful lot of stuff to do!

"Don't worry," she says. "I'll help you fill it out."

Just then, her cell phone rings. The ring sounds like a song from the KICK country radio station.

Lilly flips her phone open and says, "Hey. I'm on my way." She nods her head a lot and says, "Hmm, yeah, okay." Then she closes her phone and stuffs it in her pocket.

"I gotta scoot," Lilly says. She grabs her cheerleading bag on the way to the front door. Then she gives me a wink and says, "Let me know when you get a sponsor."

"Okay," I tell her. There is one teensy tiny problem. I have no idea what a sponsor is.

I look out the window and watch as Lilly runs down the driveway to her car.

I'm still sitting on the sofa thinking about the sponsor when T.J. comes in. He says, "Hey lil' bit, what you doin' lookin' all fancy?"

I ignore the question since I have one of my own. "T.J., what is a sponsor?" I ask.

He answers, "Someone who helps you out, you know, gives you money and stuff. Racecar drivers all get sponsors. Why?" He's looking at me funny.

I smile sweetly and say, "No reason. Just askin' so I'll know."

Now his face is all twisted up. He asks, "So you'll know what?"

"Silly!" I say. "So I'll know what a sponsor does." T.J. knows a lot, but sometimes he just doesn't pay much attention.

Chapter Four
Pa to the Rescue

I need a sponsor, and I got an idea about how to get one. To do it, I have to wait till we go to Nanny and Pa's house for Sunday dinner. I hate waiting. I keep telling myself, "First things first." But I'm in an awful big hurry to be a beauty queen!

Finally, Sunday comes. As soon as I get to Nanny and Pa's big red house after church, I see Lucy. I can't wait to change and play with her. I run inside to put on my overalls. Momma doesn't want me to get my nice clothes dirty.

When I come back outside, more cousins and aunts and uncles are there. The older girls are helping Nanny, Momma, and the aunts with the food. Pa, Daddy, and the uncles have set old doors up like tables and put folding chairs out. Lilly is fixing glasses of sweet tea.

My cousin Jake rings the old black iron dinner bell in the backyard. The kids all come running to the table. It's loaded with fried chicken, rolls, purple hull peas, mashed taters, sliced tomaters, watermelon, and homemade fruit pies. Yum!

We fix our plates, and then Pa says a blessing. Then we can dig in!

We're all laughing and eating and talking. Jake tells funny jokes. The grown-ups are all talking about boring stuff like work.

I don't pay attention until I hear the aunts talking about the Blueberry Festival. They're all wondering who will be the next queen.

"I heard Maggie Lou Butler is goin' for it," I hear Momma say. "And she is right pretty, and a nice girl too." Now I'm listening to every word, but quick as a jackrabbit, they start talking about prices at the Piggly Wiggly. Lilly turns her head toward me and smiles secretly.

After we eat, Nanny and Pa walk over to their swing. They like to sit there together just like the true sweethearts they are.

I make my way over, hoping no one else follows me.

"Hello, Kylie Jean," Pa says.

Without waiting, I say, "Pa, I got a business deal for you." I'm pretty nervous and excited about my plan. I hop up and down on one leg.

Pa smiles. "Do you now, Miss Kylie Jean?" he asks. "I guess you better tell me about it quick, before you burst your bubble from sheer excitement."

"Well," I begin, "don't you want Lickskillet Farm to be famous?"

"We're famous enough already," Nanny says.

"If you were to sponsor me in the Blueberry Festival pageant," I tell her, "I could put Lickskillet Farm on ALL of my posters. Your farm would be extra famous!"

Nanny frowns. She asks, "Did you ask your momma about this, sugar?"

I shake my head and say, "No ma'am. It is a for sure surprise."

When Pa laughs, it rumbles from deep in his belly. His eyes laugh, too. He pulls a wad of money out of his pocket. Then he tells me, "Kylie Jean, you sure are somethin' else. How much money are we talkin' about here?"

"Twenty-five dollars," I tell him. "But I'm not somethin' else. I'm goin' to be the next Blueberry Queen!"

Pa smiles and hands me the money. "Thank you, Pa," I say sweetly. I kiss his cheek. As I walk away, I stuff the money in my pocket. Then I take out my list. I can cross off "Sponsor" and "25 Dollars." I'm on my way!

Chapter Five
Fairy Garden Picture

The next thing on my list is "photo," so when I get up the next day, I start looking for my photo. I look in Momma's room for the box of pictures.

When I find the box, I dump the pictures out on the floor, so I can look at them carefully. Suddenly I hear a sound.

It sounds like a pig.

Ugly Brother is standing at the door. His pink tongue is dripping with doggie drool, and doggie drool and photos do NOT go together. I jump up and grab him by the collar.

Staring into his eyes, I tell him, "Ugly Brother, I know you came to help me be a beauty queen, but this is not the way you can help me out. You have to wait until I tell you a job to do."

Ugly Brother says, "Ruff, ruff." He knows the plan. I let go and he sits down to watch me.

I look at all of the pictures. Momma has millions of baby pictures of me, T.J., and Ugly Brother. Some of them are pretty cute. In some of them, my face is all red and squished.

I show Ugly Brother pictures of him as a bitty baby. He tries to lick one.

I quickly pull the picture away and say, "No licking! Just looking!" Then he puts his head under his paw.

There are pictures of Daddy and T.J. fishing. There are pictures of me, T.J., and Ugly Brother on Halloween, when I was dressed as a fairy princess. That would've been perfect, except that was the year T.J. went dressed as some kind of turtle. None of these pictures are right.

Suddenly an idea hits me like a brick. I need Pappy!

Pappy loves to take pictures. He even used to do it for a job. He has a black room to make pictures in and everything.

I know I'll need an extra-special outfit for my picture. I put on a pink dress with a huge pink fluffy skirt, my fairy wings from Halloween, a flower crown with long ribbons, and my white shiny shoes with tiny heels.

I look in Momma's little hand mirror.

There is strawberry jelly on my face. "Oops!" I say. I spit on my finger and wipe it off.

Then I look myself up and down and say, "Perfect!"

Ugly Brother is sitting in the doorway. He says, "Ruff, ruff."

Two barks is yes and one bark is no. That means I'm ready to go. "Momma," I yell, "I'm goin' to Pappy's house."

"All right," she calls back. "Don't get in the way, and come home for lunch."

"Yes ma'am," I holler.

Careful not to slam the door behind me, I run outside. I jump on my hot pink bike and pedal down the street.

Granny and Pappy live way down at the other end of Peachtree Lane. Their house is tall, old, and the color of the sky on a sunny day. That's where my daddy grew up.

I ring the bell at the front door. When Pappy opens the door, he smiles at me and says, "It's nice to see you, love bug. But Granny is at the garden club meeting. They're having a speaker on herbs today."

"I came to see you, Pappy," I tell him. "Can you take a special picture of me in Granny's rose garden?"

He smiles real big and
pats me on my head.
"Reckon I can," he says.
"Meet me 'round back in
the garden."

Pappy takes my picture on the swing, under the
arbor, and on the bench in front of the pink rose
bushes. The pink roses are the same color as my
pink dress.

I smile for every picture, and Pappy tells me,
"You're the prettiest girl I ever did see."

"Thanks, Pappy," I tell him.

When we're done, Pappy says, "All right, little
miss. Come back tomorrow, and we'll see how they
look."

"Don't tell a soul," I whisper. "This is top-secret beauty queen work."

He nods, waves, and goes inside the big blue house with his camera.

Chapter Six
Poster Party

When I get home from Pappy's, I ask Momma if my friends can come over. "I want to have a paintin' party after lunch," I explain.

I don't tell her that I want to make posters for the Blueberry Queen Festival. Posters are the next thing on my list.

"That's real nice, but don't you make a big mess now, Kylie Jean," Momma tells me.

"No ma'am," I say. "I sure don't want to make a big mess." Then I run into the kitchen to call all of my friends.

While I eat my chicken salad sandwich and drink my cold milk, I make a plan.

As soon as my friends get here, we will make a line. Each girl will have a job. I need to make the first poster so that we can make lots of copies of it. I have to have lots of posters, so the judges will see them and choose me as Blueberry Queen.

As soon as Momma goes out to work in the yard, I make my poster. It's pink, of course! That's my color.

In the middle of the poster is a giant blue circle with a smiley face. The blueberry is wearing a gold glitter crown. Underneath the blueberry, I write, "Vote Kylie Jean for Blueberry Queen!" Except I spell blueberry wrong and have to X it out and write it again.

At the bottom of the poster, I draw a big green tractor. Next to the tractor, in smaller letters, I write, "Sponsored by Lickskillet Farm." I had to ask Miss Clarabelle earlier how to spell sponsored.

Soon, the doorbell rings. Then I hear giggles and loud talking. I run downstairs to greet my friends.

Lucy comes in first. Then Kristy, Cara, Katie, and Daisy follow her.

Once they're all in my house, I say, "Ladies, we've got work to do." I take them up to my room and carefully shut the door behind them.

"You're about to see something amazing," I say. Then I show them the poster.

They love it!

Daisy says, "Kylie Jean, you know blue is my color. Please, please let me make the big blue circles."

"Okay," I say. "Who writes nice and pretty?" Kristy raises her hand real slow.

"This is goin' better than I planned it," I say. "Kristy, you do the writin' on the top and bottom of the poster."

Katie decides she'll make the smiley faces on the blue circles. "Why'd you make your face blue?" she asks me. "Are you supposed to be from outer space or somethin' like that?"

Cara laughs. "Silly! That there is a blueberry. Right, Kylie Jean?"

"You got it!" I say. "You're smart."

Cara says, "I'll use the glitter pen to make the sparkly crown, because I'm so smart. I'm a superstar!"

We all laugh. "I'll do the tractors," I tell them. "Let's get started."

Daisy starts making a big blue circle on one poster. Then she passes it to Kristy, who will add the writing.

I'm at the end, so I have to wait for the first poster to go all the way through the line before it gets to me.

Then I notice something. Kristy spelled the word blueberry wrong (like blubery) and put a big X over it, just like I did.

"Stop!" I yell.

"What's wrong?" Kristy asks. "I'm making it just like you did!"

I sigh. "I know," I say. "But you don't have to write it the wrong way. Spell blueberry right on all the posters. Okay?"

She nods her head yes and starts to write again.

After about an hour we have a whole pile of pink posters. Cara asks, "So, where are you gonna put all your pretty posters? If it was me, I would put one at the Piggly Wiggly grocery store."

Daisy says, "How about the Drive-N-Go?"

Katie says, "How 'bout taking them to church?"

Kristy says, "I think you should put one at the courthouse."

Lucy says, "Take some posters downtown."

We're a great team. I love my friends!

Then Momma calls, "Y'all come down. I've got hot chocolate chip cookies and ice cold lemonade."

Daisy shouts, "Yum-o!" We all run for the door.

I'm glad my posters are done. But there's so much left on my list. I don't have much time till the Blueberry Festival. I've been saving one of the hardest things for last.

I have to write an essay!

Chapter Seven

The Letter

When I wake up the next day, I get going even before I have breakfast. The first thing I have to do today is see the pictures that Pappy took. I need to pick one to send in with my application for Blueberry Queen.

I stroll over to Pappy's house. When I get there, I ring the doorbell that sounds like a church bell.

Granny comes to the door. She asks, "Are you here to see Pappy and get your pictures?"

"Yup!" I answer.

Pappy calls for me to come to the kitchen. My pictures are all on the table.

When I see them, I can't help it: I shout with joy. Then I whisper, "Pappy, you made me look sweet as an angel!"

After looking at each picture, I choose the one with the best smile.

Pappy agrees. "That's my favorite one too, little miss," he says. Then he adds, "You know I like to take your picture, so you ask me anytime."

I give my pappy some sugar and say thank you before I go.

I'm in a hurry to get home. Another project is waiting for me.

I need help on my essay. And to help me, I need someone who knows a lot of words. Maybe even a million words. Lucky for me, I know just the right person to help me.

As soon as I get home, I run upstairs to my room and find my pink notebook and my pink pen with the long feather on it.

"Momma!" I holler. "I'm goin' to Miss Clarabelle's house."

"Don't bug her," Momma says.

"I won't!" I call as I slam the front door.

I carefully run across the yard, because I do not want to step on any of the beautiful flowers. They look like a quilt tucking Miss Clarabelle's house into the green grass.

When Miss Clarabelle opens the door, she smiles.

"I need help, ma'am," I say.

She waves her hand and I follow her to the fancy living room. Miss Clarabelle calls it the parlor. Like I said, she knows a lot of words!

Miss Clarabelle sits down in a big, soft, purple chair. Then she pats the footstool in front of her. "Come and sit," she says. After I make myself comfortable, she asks me, "How can I help you, Kylie Jean?"

I explain all of my writing troubles to her and I can tell she's listening because she looks at my face when I'm talking and she nods her head at all the right times.

Then I say, "The worst part is, I need a commendation. I don't even know what one is."

She laughs. It sounds like a little tinkling bell. "Do you mean a recommendation?" she asks.

Miss Clarabelle explains that a recommendation is just a letter of kind words in support of someone. She tells me lots of folks need them to get a job. I wonder if Daddy needed one to get his job at the newspaper.

I think real hard, and my forehead gets wrinkly. I squeeze my eyes tight. Then an idea jumps right on me like a flea.

I take a deep breath. Then I say, "Miss Clarabelle, would you do me the honor of writing my recommendation to be Blueberry Queen?"

She smiles and says, "I would be delighted to write a letter supporting you as the next queen."

"I got another problem I need your help with, ma'am," I say quietly. "I have to write an essay. And it has to have three hundred words in it!"

"My goodness," Miss Clarabelle says. "That is a long essay for someone your age. But I think you can do it."

"How do I get started?" I ask.

"Well, the first thing you should do is make a list of all of the reasons you want to be Blueberry Queen," Miss Clarabelle tells me.

"My reasons are I want to be a queen, I'm right pretty, and I like blueberries," I tell her.

Miss Clarabelle laughs. "I think you may need a few more things than that," she says. "Why don't you think of about five more reasons you'll be a great Blueberry Queen. Then you can start on your essay. I'll get to work on your letter."

She starts working on my recommendation. I can hear her fancy pen scratching across the paper. While she writes, I work on my list.

When I get bored of that, I draw blueberries on the paper.

After about a hundred minutes she puts down the pen. Then she hands me the letter.

To whom it may concern:

I am writing this letter to recommend Miss Kylie Jean Carter for Blueberry Queen. I have known this young lady from the day she was born. It is her life-long goal and dream to be a queen. I have watched her work in my garden and flowerbeds, so I know she likes growing things. I also know that she works hard and is willing to get dirty if the job calls for it. She is nice and kind. Kylie Jean has many supporters, and we would love to see her at the front of the Blueberry Festival parade.

I cannot think of a better young lady to be our next Blueberry Queen. Thank you!

Yours Sincerely,

Miss Clarabelle Lee

I can feel tears prickling in my eyes as I jump up and throw my arms around her neck. I squeeze her in a big hug.

"Miss Clarabelle," I say, "you went and made me cry with your words. Your letter will make those judges choose me. I just know it for sure!"

Chapter Eight

Three Hundred Words

Back at home, I sneak up to T.J.'s room. Ugly Brother follows me and sits down beside the desk. I push all the junk off of T.J.'s desk chair and sit down. The computer is already on, so I get right to work.

First things first, I think about my list. I write all my ideas on a blank piece of paper from the printer.

I begin. I delete. I begin again. I keep writing until my essay is done. Then I read it out loud to Ugly Brother.

Why I Want to be Blueberry Queen

By Kylie Jean Carter

Ever since I was a bitty baby I knew I wanted to be a beauty queen. It is my big dream in life. Being a queen is important work. I know because I've watched Miss America every year since I was two. I know the beauty queen wave too. Nice and slow, a side to side wave. You will not find a young lady for your queen who has more sparkle than me.

I have all the right stuff to be your new Blueberry Queen. My nanny and pa are my sponsors. They own world-famous Lickskillet Farm. My pink Kylie Jean for Blueberry Queen posters are all over town. I have included a picture my pappy took of me in the rose garden.

As you can see I am wearing my flower crown, but I am sure the picture would be even better if I had a real crown to wear, so just pretend I have one on. Okay?

A lot of pretty girls will enter your beauty queen contest, but I am so very pretty. My eyes are as blue as the summer sky and my hair is long, brown, and curly. Everyone knows a beautiful smile can make a queen. Don't you worry! I always brush my teeth every day, so they are white as my momma's pearl necklace.

Speaking of my momma, she likes to say, "Kylie Jean, pretty is as pretty does." This makes me think that I have to be nice on my insides to be pretty on my outsides. I am smart and I work real hard. Plus, I try to be nice all the time.

Finally, the last thing I want to say is that I just love blueberries! I know these things will make you decide that I am the very best choice for your new queen.

When I get done reading, Ugly Brother says, "Ruff, ruff." That means he thinks it is really good. I'm glad.

After I finish my essay, I look at the next thing on my list. I need to get some transportation. I'm thinking about using my pink bike, but it will be hard to hold the handlebars and wave real pretty to the crowd.

I can tell Ugly Brother thinks it is a bad idea too, so I ask him. I say, "Ugly Brother, do you think I should ride my bike in the parade?"

He says, "Ruff." That means no.

All of a sudden an idea hits my brain like dew on grass.

"Ugly Brother," I say, "I'm surely goin' to need your help."

He says, "Ruff, ruff." That means yes!

Ugly Brother follows me to the garage. I pull out my old red wagon and a small stool. I put the stool inside the wagon. Then I climb inside the wagon and wave nice and slow, side to side.

This just might work!

Ugly Brother puts his face under his paw and whines. He seems nervous.

"Don't worry, Ugly Brother," I say. "I'm not done yet."

Next I go inside. I get one of Momma's old blue sheets, a pair of scissors, and a blue pillow off of T.J.'s bed. I cut the sheet so I can put it over the stool and wagon. Then I cut a big round hole in the center of the dark blue pillow.

I look at Ugly Brother and say, "When I get through with you, you're gonna look just like a big ole blueberry."

Ugly Brother puts his other paw over his face and whines louder. I sit down on the ground beside him.

"You're not gonna like this," I tell him, "but face it, you're not so handsome, Ugly Brother. This is gonna make you look real nice."

It takes me a long time, but I finally get the pillow pulled up around his middle. Ugly Brother stands real still. The blue pillow is like a giant blue inner tube around his middle.

He has white pillow stuffing stuck to his pink tongue, and one of his ears is bent back from me pushing him into the pillow.

I shake my head and put my hands on my hips. "It's your own fault you got stuffin' on your tongue," I tell him. "You should have put it in your mouth."

He tries to sit down, but the pillow gets in the way.

"No sitting down on the job, Ugly Brother," I scold him. "You have to pull this wagon." I tie him up to the handle of the wagon.

Then I shout, "Go to Granny and Pappy's house, Ugly Brother!" He starts to pull me, real slow like. I smile and wave.

I think I have sunburn by the time we get to the end of the street. We've been moving slow as molasses. Ugly Brother has had several resting times along the way. I don't think he will make it down all the streets on the day of the parade.

Granny and Pappy are sitting on their porch. I wave when I get closer.

Pappy says, "Kylie Jean, just what are you doin' to that poor dog? And what is he wearin'?"

"I need transportation," I explain. "And my transportation is wearin' a blueberry costume."

Granny runs inside the house and then comes back with a bowl of cold water for Ugly Brother. She says, "He must be burnin' up dressed up like that, poor boy."

She starts to laugh again and has tears in her eyes. "Pappy, come help us get this pillow off of this dog!" she says.

After he gets Ugly Brother out of the pillow, Pappy looks me in the eye. "Listen, love bug," he says. "If they pick you for Blueberry Queen, I have a fancy old car that will make it down the street better than Ugly Brother here."

I can't believe it! "Yippee!" I shout.

Then I look to make sure no one else but Granny and Pappy heard me shouting. I hug Pappy real hard.

He asks, "Is that the best bear hug you've got?"

"Yup!" I tell him, but I squeeze him even tighter.

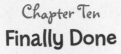

Chapter Ten
Finally Done

On Wednesday morning, I wake up early. The house is full up with the smell of blueberry muffins. Momma must be trying another new recipe for the Blueberry Bake-Off. She only has a few days left before the festival.

Every year since I can remember, my momma has won a blue first-place ribbon for her cooking. She has the ribbons pinned all over the inside of our pantry door.

I stretch. I yawn. The sun is up, and today is going to be a great day.

My plan is to finish my beauty queen list.

Suddenly an idea hits my brain like chocolate syrup on ice cream. Maybe my list is all done!

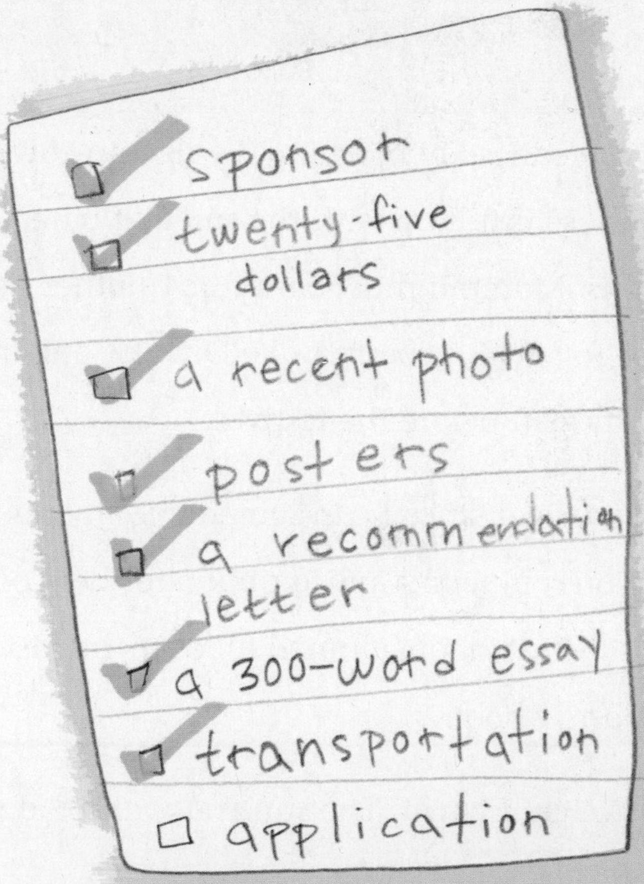

- ☑ sponsor
- ☑ twenty-five dollars
- ☑ a recent photo
- ☑ posters
- ☑ a recommendation letter
- ☑ a 300-word essay
- ☑ transportation
- ☐ application

I can check off everything on my list but the application. I shout, "Yippee!"

Ugly Brother agrees. He says, "Ruff, ruff."

Before I even get dressed, I go downstairs to get the phone and call Lilly. At first, I can't find the phone. After I look all over the den, I find it in the couch cushions. This means T.J. was talking on the phone. He never puts it back on the charger. I dial Lilly's cell phone.

Lilly answers. "Hey girl, what's up?" She's getting ready to go to cheer camp, so I make it quick.

"Lilly, my list is done!" I tell her. "I have everything you told me to get. Do you have my application ready?"

I hear Lilly slamming her car door. She asks, "Do you have a sponsor?"

"Sure do," I say. "Nanny and Pa."

Lilly laughs and says, "Good job, little cousin. Are you sure you have everything on the list?"

"Yes!" I tell her.

Lilly tells me that she will come by in the afternoon to pick up all of my papers and send my application. I'm really on my way to being the Blueberry Queen!

Chapter Eleven
An Extra-Elegant Dress

After dinner, it's time to tell Momma my big news. I go to the kitchen. Momma is doing dishes in her apron with the blueberries on it.

"Momma, I have a surprise," I say. "I've been workin' on something you don't know about. Nanny, Pa, T.J., Ugly Brother, Lilly, Lucy, Granny, Pappy, and my friends all helped me send in my papers to be the Blueberry Queen."

Momma's eyes get big, and she sits down in a chair at the kitchen table. She says, "Well I do declare, Kylie Jean, that is a big surprise!"

I sit beside Momma and tell her all about the pageant. She looks at me and smiles. Then she says, "Honey, you are going to need a dress. We will need your granny to help us pick one out. I better call her and see if she can go with us tomorrow."

The next day we go to Jefferson to buy my dress at the Elegance Dress Shop. It takes a long time to drive to Jefferson, but I'm gonna need an extra-special elegant dress. On the way, Momma tells Granny all about the tasty blueberry treats she has been making and how she is after another blue ribbon this year.

When we turn onto Old Jacksonville Road, I know we are getting close. Every bit of me is on edge with excitement.

Then Momma says to Granny, "Let's go to Ms. Pauline's Tearoom and eat lunch first."

I can't believe it! How can they be thinking about eating lunch now? We are almost there.

Momma's van pulls right into the tearoom parking lot. Ms. Pauline has her tearoom in a big old house. Granny says, "I just love the chicken salad here." The last thing I can think about is eating. I want to pick out my dress!

We go inside the old house and sit at a table. The waitress comes and takes our order. We all have chicken salad sandwiches with fresh fruit. I have milk, but the grown-ups have sweet tea.

I eat fast, but Momma and Granny take their time. While I wait, I look around and see lots of ladies with big tea hats.

Usually going to Ms. Pauline's is a special treat, but today I would have rather had a Happy Meal if it meant we'd get my dress right away.

Our next stop is the Elegance Dress Shop. Out front there's a big fancy sign with letters that have lots of curls on them. The shop sells a lot of fancy dresses for weddings and parties.

We go inside, and I go to the dressing room. It is big, with a red velvety chair in the corner. I stand there in my slip. Beauty queens always wear a slip because it is classy.

Momma and Granny help me try on about one hundred dresses. I feel like a Barbie doll, the way they keep putting new dresses on me. We try white ones with ruffles, yellow ones the color of soft creamy butter, and a blue one with bows.

There is a big mirror with three pieces of glass. When I stand in the middle, I can see all around me. I twirl in the blue dress.

Granny frowns. She says, "I just don't think we have the right dress yet. You look right pretty, but somehow it just doesn't seem like a winning dress."

Momma agrees. "We best take one more look at the rack."

I keep twirling in front of the mirror.

Finally, Granny brings one more dress for me to try on. It is a light pink color, and it has little white dots all over it. It has white lace, a big white satin bow, and fluffy white net slip to wear under it.

When I come out wearing it, Momma and Granny are speechless because I look so beautiful in my dress.

"I feel like a real true beauty queen wearin' this dress," I tell them.

Momma says, "I think we found the one."

Granny says, "Yes, we surely did!"

I smile and twirl around and around. Momma buys me the dress and some tights with little white dots and gloves with white lace. Now I'm ready for my big day at the pageant!

Chapter Twelve
The Blueberry Festival

The next day, I'm helping Momma get ready to take her special blueberry pecan granola pie to the festival. My pageant won't be until tomorrow. We load up three big baskets with pies. T.J. carries them to the van.

Momma calls, "Y'all, get in the van."

Ugly Brother has trouble jumping up. He barks and jumps. He gets his front end up, but not his back end. He can't do it, so he covers his face with his paws. I think he's embarrassed.

Daddy picks up Ugly Brother and puts him in the back. We drive as close as we can to the town square. Some of the streets downtown are closed. We are still two blocks from the festival. "We're gonna have to walk," Daddy says.

We all get out of the van and start to walk. We walk past shops, coffee houses, jewelry stores, and the bank. I'm the only one not carrying a pie basket, but I have Ugly Brother's leash.

As we get closer T.J. shouts, "The Blueberry Brothers Bluegrass Band sounds awesome! I just love that banjo playing. Hey, could I sell my guitar and get a banjo?"

Momma says, "T.J., you cannot sell Pa's guitar, but if you have enough saved up then go right on and buy yourself a banjo."

Momma is walking fast. She's worried about being late for the bake-off. Daddy is in a hurry too. He wants to head over to the blueberry pancake breakfast.

We turn the corner and see little white tents all over the place. There are tents selling blueberry jellies, jams, and barbecue sauce. There are tents selling blueberries by the bucket and blueberry plants in big pots. There are tents for contests and events, too. I even see a face-painting tent run by the cheerleaders. Lilly is there. She sees me and waves.

Momma points to one tent and says, "There's the bake-off tent."

Daddy says, "We can drop off these pies and go eat breakfast."

T.J. nods. He says, "I'll eat pancakes right now, but later I'm going to enter the Blue Face Pie-Eating Contest for sure!"

By now, Ugly Brother is pulling me. He is so excited to see all the folks that he keeps trying to run over and say hi to them all. I see Nanny and Pa sitting at a picnic table. They're with Granny and Pappy. Lucy is with them!

My relatives all wave, and I try to wave back, but I need both my hands on the leash now because Ugly Brother is pulling so hard.

We leave the pies at the bake-off tent and go to get our pancakes.

Then we sit with my grandparents and Lucy and eat. Daddy and T.J. eat three plates of blueberry pancakes each.

Some of the blueberries are small as a dime. Some of the pancakes are big as the plate.

The grown-ups are all talking. I can tell Momma is as nervous as a cat in a pool. Cats don't like water one little bit. I don't think I should say how I know.

Lucy asks, "Did you see your pink posters hanging by the courthouse?"

"Yup," I answer. "They look awesome!" I'm finished with my pancakes. "Momma and Daddy, can Lucy and I go run around and have fun?" I ask.

"All by yourselves?" Momma says. "I don't know."

Pa wipes syrup off his face. "I'll go with 'em," he says.

"Yay!" I say. "Let's go!" I grab one of Pa's hands. Lucy grabs the other.

We spend our time visiting all the little tents and getting our faces painted. I get blueberries on my face. Lucy gets them too!

"You girls look right pretty," the face-painting lady tells us.

"Why thank you!" I say.

I love the Blueberry Festival. It is so much fun! I wish it could happen every day during the summer.

Finally, it's time to see who the winner of the bake-off is. We go back to the tables.

Daddy is holding Momma's hand. Momma looks nervous, so I give her a wink. She winks back at me.

Before long, a man in a white suit and cowboy hat steps up to face the crowd. Pa whispers to me, "That man there is the head judge."

The man shouts, "We have the results! Shelly is the winner for her delicious blueberry pecan granola pie."

Shelly is my momma's name! We all cheer and clap for my momma.

Nanny says, "I declare, this is the tenth year in a row you've been number one. You are some cook!"

"She sure is," Daddy says.

Momma jumps up to get her picture taken with the blue ribbon. Today it will sit by her pie so everybody can see it.

I tell Lucy, "Tomorrow, Momma will put her ribbon on the pantry door. You know what else will happen tomorrow?"

Lucy shakes her head. "What?" she asks.

I raise my head proudly and tell her, "Tomorrow, I will be the new Blueberry Queen."

Chapter Thirteen

Time to Shine!

The day of the pageant is finally here. At five o'clock in the morning, I wake up because I can't sleep any more. Then I'm so excited that I can't eat my breakfast.

My stomach feels like T.J.'s pet hamster is running around in it.

When I go downstairs, Momma says, "Kylie Jean, sugar, eat some toast. You don't want to feel sick at the pageant."

"Too late, Momma!" I say. "I already feel sick!"

Momma laughs. She says, "Eat your toast. Just remember, soon-to-be beauty queens do not get nervous."

After I eat my toast, I take a long bubble bath and scrub under my nails and behind my ears. Then I get dressed. First I put on my white tights, then my fluffy white slip, and finally my pretty new pink dress.

Granny and Nanny have come to help me. Nanny buckles my little shiny pink shoes with the tiny heels. Granny pulls my hair back in a princess style.

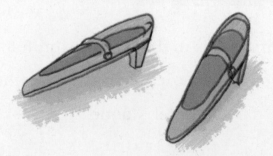

I look in my mirror and see a soon-to-be Blueberry Queen.

Downstairs, everyone is waiting to see me. When I walk in the kitchen, Daddy, Pappy, Pa, T.J., and Ugly Brother all gather around me. I twirl around so they can see my beautiful dress.

Ugly Brother says, "Ruff, ruff."

Daddy says, "Well, sweetheart, don't you look all grown up!"

"She sure does," Pappy says. He looks at the kitchen clock and adds, "We better hit the road or our little miss will be late."

My family gets in the van. The grandparents all ride in Pappy's old car. I feel dizzy the whole way downtown to the Hotel Magnolia.

When we pull in the parking lot, there are about a million cars parked all around the hotel. Daddy helps me get out of the van, and Momma holds my hand.

Normally I would skip all the way inside, but not today. I'm trying to act like a true queen, so I stand straight and tall.

Pa holds the door open and we go inside. The ballroom is right next to us. You should see all the people in there! It is packed full.

Momma takes me to wait in the room next to the ballroom with all the other girls who want to be the Blueberry Queen.

Then I notice something. Everyone else waiting is a grown-up girl! I can't believe it! They are all so fancy.

Maggie Lou Butler is standing right beside me. Her blond hair is fixed up on top of her head. She looks just like a movie star. All these older girls look like movie stars.

I start to get the hiccups. I always get them when I'm scared.

"You just wait a minute, Kylie Jean, you'll be fine," Momma says. "Take a big breath. Remember, this is your dream come true."

Momma is right. In a minute they will call our names, and we will go out and introduce ourselves.

Momma smiles and whispers to me, "Smile, talk slow, and be clear, so they can understand you."

Then I hear a voice. "Kylie Jean Carter." That's me!

I walk into the ballroom and up on the stage. But the microphone is as tall as my momma, and I can't reach.

Everyone laughs. I don't know what to do. I could yell, but that's not how beauty queens act. It wouldn't be right. Luckily, a man runs out and fixes the microphone so I can talk.

"Hello, y'all," I begin. "My name is Kylie Jean Carter, and my sponsor is Lickskillet Farm. Ever since I was a bitty baby, I've been wantin' to be a queen. Please vote for me for your next Blueberry Queen."

Then I wave nice and slow, side to side, the beauty queen wave. I smile real big, too.

Everybody laughs again. Not like they're making fun of me, but like I make them happy.

Then I go and stand in the back of the stage next to Momma. About ten grown-up girls walk out and tell their names. Then we all have to wait to see who the new queen is going to be.

I just know it is going to be me!

Pretty soon, a man comes out on the stage. "Who's that?" I ask Momma.

"That's the head judge," Momma whispers back. "He's going to tell us who the winner is!"

I hold my breath as the man says, "I have the results. It was a very close contest this year."

I feel sorry for those grown-up girls. They're going to be awful sad when I win.

Then the judge announces, "Maggie Lou Butler from Prickly Pear Creek is our new Blueberry Queen!"

Maggie Lou goes to the stage. Everyone is clapping. Momma pats my back.

I think I might cry.

Then the clapping stops. The judge man has something else to say. He looks over at me and says, "For the very first time ever, we have a Little Miss Blueberry Queen. Kylie Jean Carter, come on up here!"

Everyone goes wild! They're all cheering and calling my name. Momma starts crying, so I pat her back. Then I skip all the way to the microphone. The man puts a diamond tiara on my head.

I wave to everyone again. Nice and slow, side to side. For the first time, I'm not just pretending I'm a real, true queen.

I am one.

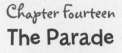

Chapter Fourteen
The Parade

The day after the pageant, I'm going to be in a parade. I eat a huge breakfast with my family.

Momma says, "Kylie Jean, finish your eggs so you can get dressed."

After T.J. finishes his breakfast, he goes to help Pappy shine up the fancy old car.

Daddy winks at me. "I have a special job to do today," he says.

I look at Momma, but she just shrugs. Daddy is up to something. I just know it.

Momma smiles and says, "When you wear that tiara, you will feel real special."

I get dressed in my special pink dress again. Momma fixes my hair back and puts my tiara on. Then I'm ready to go for a ride in the parade.

Daddy is waiting downstairs. He hands me a big box with a giant bow on the top.

"What is it, Daddy?" I ask.

"Open it and see," he tells me with a wink.

I open up the box. Inside, I find a big ole bunch of pink roses.

Daddy smiles and says, "A queen needs roses, Kylie Jean."

"Oh, Daddy!" I say. "I'm gonna smile and wave and make y'all proud of me."

"We couldn't be any prouder of you than we already are, Kylie Jean," Momma tells me.

I hold the flowers in front of me and wave. Then I ask Ugly Brother, "Do I look like a queen?"

He says, "Ruff, ruff." That means yes!

Out front, Pappy honks the horn of his fancy old car. We all go outside. Pa puts a white fake fur blanket on the back of Pappy's car and lifts me up to sit on it.

I fluff out my skirt and fix my roses. Pa says, "You sure are somethin', Kylie Jean."

I tell him, "I'm not somethin', I'm a Little Miss Blueberry Queen."

Pa smiles. He leans over and taps me on the nose. Then he asks, "Ready, sugar pie?"

"Yes, sir, I surely am," I answer. "Ever since I was a bitty baby."

Pa, Pappy, Daddy, and T.J. get in the car. Pappy drives down our street and turns onto Main Street. I see Miss Clarabelle waving her fan at me. All of my friends are calling my name. Nanny, Granny, and Momma are all blowing kisses to me as I pass by. Ugly Brother is sitting by Momma with his new blue collar, saying, "Ruff, ruff!" to me.

I think I may need a fan club after today.

Being the Little Miss Blueberry Queen made me happier and prouder than anything. Someday I'm going to be a real true beauty queen. I have big plans!

Singing Queen

Table of Contents

Chapter One
Summertime

Early in the morning, the sun is already hot as a firecracker when Momma's van pulls up in front of a tiny brick building.

I'm wearing my old red and white striped one-piece swimsuit. That's because today, Momma is letting me swim at the city pool with my friend Cara.

It only costs a dollar to get in for the whole day! Can you believe it?

Before I get out, Momma turns around in the front seat. "Did you bring a towel and sunscreen in your bag? How about change for snacks?" she asks.

I hold up the beach bag covered in pink and white anchors and answer, "Yes, ma'am. And I have some quarters from my piggy bank."

"You better be good and do what the lifeguard tells you. You hear?" Momma tells me.

"Don't worry," I say. "I'll be good, Momma." Then I climb out of the van, dragging my bag along with me to the sidewalk. I slip off my flip-flops and pretend I'm walking on hot coals like they do at the circus.

At the window, I pay my dollar to get in. Then I shove open the big metal gate.

As soon as I walk through, I see the pool! It's a giant circle of water the color of bright blue Jell-O.

I start looking for Cara right off. She's not in one of the long chairs. Those are filled with older girls trying to get a tan. There's a tall chair with a lifeguard.

I know him. His name is Wes. He's my brother T.J.'s friend, and he makes you follow the pool rules.

Right in front of the lifeguard's stand is a tiny round baby pool. Mommies sit all along the edge holding their little kids. The babies kick their legs while the mommies talk.

I see Cara in the shallow end of the pool. She waves and shouts, "Hey, Kylie Jean, I'm over here!"

I jump into the pool. The warm water laps against my face as I swim over to Cara. "Let's play mermaid!" she says.

First, I pretend to swish my long mermaid tail. Really, it's just my legs twisted together. Then Cara swishes her tail too.

After a while, I climb out of the pool and stand on the edge.

I yell, "Look at me! Cannonball!"

I take three giant steps back. Then I run toward the pool. As I jump into the deep end, I tuck myself into a tiny ball.

Whoosh!

Water splashes everywhere. It rains fat little drops all over the older girls sunbathing in their bikinis.

"I'll never get a good tan if you keep on getting me wet!" one of them yells.

"No more cannonballs!" another one says.

I dog paddle over to Cara, and we both laugh. She gives me a high five.

Then she says, "That was your best one yet! If your splash was any bigger you'd hit the lifeguard and get in trouble."

I nod. "He'd tell T.J. and T.J. would tell Momma," I say. Then I have a really great idea of something fun we can do at the pool.

"Hey, you wanna dive for quarters?" I ask.

"Sure!" Cara says.

I run over to my pool bag and find some of my shiny new quarters. Then I hop back into the water — no cannonball this time — and hang on to the side of the pool.

I drop the coins.

Cara says, "Ready . . . set . . . go!"

We dive in.

The coins spiral down through the blue water like shiny fish bait. Wiggling through the water like tadpoles, we swim after the silvery treasure. After a minute, Cara swims up for air. I do too. Then we dive back down and finally find the quarters.

Afterward, we float on our backs for a while.

"I love summertime," I say.

"Me too," Cara says. Then she asks, "Hey! Are you goin' to the Fourth of July Jubilee on Saturday?"

"Yup!" I say. "We always do. Granny is makin' jewelry for the craft show, and Momma always makes a real big picnic for my whole family to eat. I love the Jubilee!"

"Me too," Cara says. "I just love summer."

"I do too," I tell her.

"They're havin' a talent show this year at the Jubilee," Cara tells me. "It's gonna be just like American Idol, but not as big, since only folks from our town will be in it."

Right then, an idea hits my brain like ketchup on French fries!

I bet I could do a talent in the talent show!

"How old do you have to be to be in the show?" I ask.

Cara shrugs. "I dunno," she says. "Nobody told me any of the rules."

My mind is spinning faster than a fan blade on a hot August day.

I like the pool, but I have work to do now!

I swim to the side of the pool and climb out, dripping water as I walk over to my pink towel and my beach bag.

"I gotta go home now," I tell Cara. "Are you coming to the pool tomorrow?"

She laughs and splashes some water at me. "Yes," she says. "I'm going to come every day until school starts again, unless it's raining. See you tomorrow!"

Waving goodbye, I drag my pool bag and pink towel to the pool gate.

Chapter Two
Big News

I run home as fast as I can, dragging my big ole beach bag behind me. I speed down the street and take a shortcut through Granny and Pappy's yard. They won't mind.

The air smells like green grass. Pappy is out mowing the lawn.

"How's my girl?" he shouts when he sees me.

I just wave back. I don't have time to stop and chat.

I have to concentrate on how I can find out about the contest.

When I pass Miss Clarabelle's driveway, I see her newspaper lying on the ground. This gives me an idea! Newspapers have lots of things in them, and I bet one of the things in this newspaper is the rules about the talent show at the Fourth of July Jubilee.

When I run up our driveway, Ugly Brother and the paper are both waiting for me.

"Can you help me find out about the Jubilee?" I ask Ugly Brother.

He runs over to me and barks, "Ruff, ruff!"

Two barks means yes!

"Thanks, Ugly Brother," I say.

Together, we sit in the grass under the shade of a big oak tree and look at the newspaper.

"Do you think I can find out about the Jubilee in the paper?" I ask Ugly Brother.

He barks, "Ruff, ruff." Two barks again! Ugly Brother and I are on the right track.

I tear the plastic wrapper off of the paper. Then a breeze blows the paper open.

When I look up, I notice that the sky is gray. It looks like it might rain. The pages of the newspaper keep flipping in the wind. Ugly Brother decides to help me out by standing on one side of the paper while I look at the other side.

Before I look for the Jubilee, I read the comics. Those comics are so funny! Ugly Brother likes the one with the big orange cat who eats everything. That's his favorite. My favorite is one with a lot of kids who live in a house and like to run all over their neighborhoods all the time.

We are busy laughing together when it starts to rain.

There is a teeny tiny clap of thunder. Then it's like a river falls out of the sky and we both get soaking wet.

I take off for the porch, yelling, "Hurry, Ugly Brother! The paper will get wet!"

He follows me, dragging my pool bag and towel. He is not a very fast runner like me.

It's too late to save the paper. The pages are a damp smudgy mess.

I sit down on the porch floor. Ugly Brother plops down right next to me.

"I guess we'll need a new plan," I say.

My daddy works at the newspaper. Maybe he'll bring me home a new copy.

"Should I call Daddy?" I ask Ugly Brother. "I just know he could bring me the newspaper when he comes home from work. Right?"

Ugly Brother turns his head to the side and barks, "Ruff!"

One bark means no. "You're right," I say. "That's way too long to wait. Daddy won't be home from work until five-thirty."

I think about it for a while longer while the rain falls down outside.

The answer hits my brain like rain on a polka-dotted umbrella. Granny will know all about the rules. Granny knows about everything for the Jubilee.

I run into the house and straight to the phone in the kitchen.

I dial Granny's number. I know it by heart. Granny answers. She knows it's me as soon as I say hello.

"Hello, Kylie Jean. What are you doing today?" asks Granny.

"Oh, I went to the pool with Cara this morning," I tell her.

"That sounds fun," Granny says. "Today was a good day for the pool, before it started raining. Nice and hot out. What did you do with your friend?"

"We dove for quarters and played mermaid," I say. "And she told me they're putting on a talent show at the Jubilee this year."

"That's right, they sure are!" Granny says. "It should be a great show."

"Can you tell me all about the contest? Pretty please?" I say. "I know you'll be at the Jubilee craft show selling your jewelry."

Granny laughs. She says, "You can just go right on down to Jacksonville City Hall and sign up for the show."

"Only if they let kids sign up," I say.

"That's right, darlin'," Granny says.

"Do you know if they do?" I ask nervously. "Cara didn't know if kids could be in it."

"Hmm," Granny says. "Well, I just don't know. I hope so, because you sure are a talented little girl, and I'd love to see you in the Jubilee talent show. Miss June at City Hall will know all of the rules."

"Thanks, Granny," I say. "I better get moving!"

After I hang up, I look at Ugly Brother. "That was just the first part of my plan," I tell him. "We need to get an umbrella and take a walk for part two."

He barks twice. Ugly Brother likes this plan.

My big umbrella is right by the front door. I step outside and pop it open. Ugly Brother is still waiting inside. He doesn't like getting wet.

"Come on," I say. "I got the big umbrella so we both can fit under it."

"Ruff, ruff!" Ugly Brother says. Then the two of us head off down the street under the giant umbrella.

Chapter Three
City Hall Sign Up

On our way to City Hall, the rain stops.
Right away, it starts to get hot out. Real hot. I'm
sweating inside my rubber boots and raincoat, so
we stop to get a Sno-ball.

The roof on the Sno-ball stand looks like a huge
rainbow-flavored Sno-ball. Inside the Sno-ball
there is only room for one person.

Ugly Brother and I stand in line, waiting for our
turn. It's a long line. I count the people in front of
us.

One, two, three, four, five, six. We have a long time to wait!

The first person in line orders a lemon twist Sno-ball. The next two people order rainbow-flavored Sno-balls. I don't hear the rest because I am too busy talking to Ugly Brother.

I ask him, "Do you want your usual flavor?"

He barks, "Ruff, ruff."

"Okay. Grape for you and cotton candy for me," I say.

When it's our turn, I order. The teenage boy who's working hands me one pink and one purple Sno-ball. I pay with some quarters from my pocket.

I put the purple Sno-ball on the ground for Ugly Brother. He slurps and grunts, enjoying the frozen treat. The pink one is for me.

We start walking.

My tongue is pink, but Ugly Brother's is purple like a grape. The Sno-ball is nice and cold. It feels good in the heat.

I have one bite left as we walk up to City Hall. City Hall isn't really a hall, not like the hall in my house, anyway. It's really just a big ole white house downtown near the county courthouse.

I suck down the last sweet goodness of my cotton candy Sno-ball. Then I tie Ugly Brother up to the bicycle stand right in front of Jacksonville City Hall.

"You be good and no barking. Okay?" I tell him. He whines and sits down. I know he wants to come with me, but most places don't let dogs come inside. I don't know why.

Inside City Hall, the air is ice cold. My boots squish across the floor all the way over to Miss June's desk. Squish, squish, squish.

I look behind me and see that I'm leaving some wet footprints on the floor. I hope that Miss June doesn't mind!

Miss June hears me coming and looks up.

"Well, hello there!" she says. "How are you doing, Kylie Jean?" she asks. "And how about your big brother and your momma and daddy? Are you gettin' excited for the Jubilee?"

"Yes ma'am,
I am," I say.
"And we're
all fine, thank
you." Then I
ask, "I need
some help. How
old do you have
to be to sign up
for the Jubilee
talent show?"

Miss June doesn't say anything. Instead, she offers me a red and white striped peppermint stick from her candy jar.

I remember my manners and say, "Thank you, ma'am."

She says, "You're welcome. I need to make a quick call to find out the answer to your question. Okay?"

"Yes ma'am," I say.

Miss June punches a number into the phone and starts talking real quietly.

I snap the candy stick in half. Pop!

I'm saving part of it for Ugly Brother as a treat for being good outside while he waits for me.

After a long time, Miss June finally hangs up the phone.

"It seems we didn't really put anything in the rules about age," she tells me. "If you are old enough to have talent, you're in."

She hands me a clipboard.

Then she adds, "Good thing you came today since it's the last day to sign up. Just write your name, talent, and how long you'll be on the stage."

I bite my lip. Then I admit, "I'm not sure just yet what I'll be doing or for how long."

Miss June smiles. She says, "Just put down your name for now."

"All right," I say. "I'll be back tomorrow to put down the rest."

Then I head back outside, my boots squishing against the floor.

Outside, the sky is bright blue and it seems even hotter than before. Pa always says in Texas it can rain one minute and shine the next.

Ugly Brother has wiggled loose to look in the window for me. What a naughty boy!

I throw up my hands. "Ugly Brother, I brought you half my candy and here you are being a bad boy!" I say, grabbing his collar. "I told you to stay where I put you!"

He looks a little sad.

"Next time I tell you to stay, you better stay, or no candy for you. Okay? You got it, mister? And I mean it!" I say. Then I hand him his half of my candy stick.

He barks twice as he chomps down the candy stick in one bite. Then I tell him all about what Miss June said.

Ugly Brother seems excited, but I'm starting to get nervous.

Tomorrow I have to decide on my talent.

As we walk home, I make a list in my head.

There are lots of things I can do. I can think of a whole bunch of talents.

I can dance.

I can twirl a baton.

I can do a real good beauty-queen wave.

I can hop on one foot for a really long time, and I can turn cartwheels.

I can paint real pretty pictures.

I could read poetry or act or sing or do doggie tricks.

That last one might not work, since Ugly Brother would be the talented one, and his name isn't on the list. I didn't even think to ask if dogs are allowed in the talent show.

Besides, sometimes Ugly Brother is just too lazy to be talented!

I decide to go across the street and play with Cole and think about my talent later. Sometimes resting your brain makes it think better.

Chapter Four
Sing or Dance?

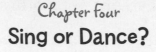

After thinking about my talent all night, I decide I should do either singing or dancing. But I need another opinion.

Momma always says two heads are better than one. So after I swim at the pool with Cara and my best cousin, Lucy, I stop by Granny and Pappy's house.

When I walk into their big blue house, I see that Pappy is in his La-Z-Boy chair watching golf on TV.

"Granny's on the sun-porch," he says. "You go on back and find her, sugar."

On the sun-porch, Granny has boxes and boxes of beads in every color on a long table. They are so pretty! They look like candy.

"Hello, Kylie Jean!" Granny says. "Have a seat."

I sit down and look at the beads. Granny asks, "Did you come to help me make jewelry for the Jubilee?"

"Sort of," I say. Then I hold up a handful of sparkly beads that look like diamonds. "I love this bling!" I tell Granny. "I'll help you, and you can help me."

Granny smiles. "All right," she says. "What do you need help with?"

"I need help decidin'. Should I sing or dance at the talent show?" I ask.

Granny keeps working on a necklace. It has strands of red beads and white beads. They look just like red and white stripes in her lap. I start working too. I'm planning on making a blingy bracelet.

Granny says, "I think you should sing."

"But what song?" I ask.

Granny thinks for a while.

Then she smiles and says, "The Star-Spangled Banner would be just perfect."

I get excited! I shout, "That's a great idea. I just gotta learn all the words by heart!" Then I add, "I better go tell Miss June right now."

"Be careful!" Granny yells as I dash toward the back door.

"Okay!" I yell back. Then I start running.

I skip all the way down to City Hall. My flip-flops squeak over the floor as I walk to Miss June's desk.

She smiles when she sees me coming and asks, "You're back! Did you figure out your talent?"

"Yes ma'am," I say. "I'm singing The Star-Spangled Banner!"

Chapter Five
Stars and Stripes Singer

When I wake up on Wednesday, I realize that I only have a few days to learn my song for the talent show.

I throw off the covers and scoot out of bed. Ugly Brother whines and sticks his nose farther under my blankets. He's not ready to get up. But the Jubilee is on Saturday, so we have to get going.

"You better get up or you can't go with me to the library after breakfast," I warn him.

He rolls over and jumps sleepily off the bed while I get dressed in my red and white striped sundress. I brush my hair. Then I brush my teeth.

Downstairs in the kitchen, I fix my own breakfast. First I get a bowl and a spoon. Next I have to choose my cereal. I like Fruity Rings and Chocolate Toasty Os. I hold up both of the boxes.

"Which one?" I ask.

Ugly Brother jumps up, trying to lick the box of Fruity Rings.

"How did you know which cereal I wanted?" I ask happily.

I sprinkle a couple of Fruity Rings on the floor for him to eat. Crunch. Crunch. Crunch.

Then I pour some in my bowl. Before I can get the milk out, T.J. comes in. He pours some Chocolate Toasty Os in Momma's biggest mixing bowl.

"Are you mowing lawns today?" I ask him while he pours milk into his bowl.

T.J.'s lawn-mowing business really keeps him busy in the summer. He mows lawns for Mrs. Bates, the Parkers, Miss Clarabelle, Daddy's boss at the paper, and the Millers.

"Yep. I have a few to mow today," he tells me, eating fast. "What are you going to do today?"

"I'm going to the library to get a book of songs, so I can learn my song for the Jubilee talent show," I say.

T.J. shoves the last bite of cereal in his mouth. Then he winks and says, "Pick a good one, so you can win it." He puts on his Texas Rangers cap and scoots out the door.

As soon as I finish my Fruity Rings, I head on over to the library. Ugly Brother comes along. We take our time walking slowly along Peach Tree Lane.

When we turn down Main Street, I wave at the mailman and the old men sitting in front of the barbershop. Then we stop right in front of the library.

"Sit! You stay right here," I tell Ugly Brother.

He barks, "Ruff, ruff."

I head inside.

When I ring the little bell on the checkout counter, Ms. Patrick, the librarian, hurries over. She asks, "What are you up to now, Kylie Jean?"

"I need the words to The Star-Spangled Banner," I tell her. "The book I get has to have all of the words. Can you please help me? Do you have a songbook like that?"

Ms. Patrick nods. "Follow me," she says.

She stops in front of one shelf and pulls out a picture book. I take it and start turning through the pages. It's cool, but the words are too spread out.

I hand it back, shaking my head. "I sure am sorry, ma'am, but I need the words all on one page. This book has a little of the words on each page."

Ms. Patrick slides the book back on the shelf. Then she whispers, "Follow me. I have just the book you're looking for."

When she hands me the next book, it is just what I need! All the words are on one page in the back of the book. "This is perfect," I tell her.

After I check out the book with my library card, I go outside and sit on the library steps. Ugly Brother and I look at the words to the song.

There are four verses. I know the first one, but in the other three, the words are really big ones to learn by heart.

Then an idea hits my brain like ants at picnic. I can just sing the first verse three times.

We go straight home without waving to anyone, so I can start to practice my song.

I sing it while I help Momma fold the towels. Then I sing it while I help Miss Clarabelle weed the flower beds. She sings with me, too!

Later I sing all the way to the pool. While we swim, my friends listen to me sing it over and over. Soon they're singing it too.

When I get home, I head straight to my room to change.

I sing all the way up the stairs and while I'm putting my play clothes on. Ugly Brother sings, too.

Then someone bangs on my door. T.J. shouts, "I can't hear my music with all your howling!"

"Okay," I say. "Sorry!" But I whisper the song two more times.

After dinner, Daddy wants to hear my song. I sit in his lap to sing to him.

I tell him, "Just listen to me. I know all the words. You have to wait, cause I'm gonna sing it three times. Okay?"

Daddy gives me a big

squeezy hug. "Okay, baby girl. Sing your song for me right now," he says.

I start singing. But it has been a long, busy day. The words to my song start to float away from me. Daddy kisses me on the cheek and carries me upstairs to bed. I am one sleepy little singer.

Chapter Six
Glitter Girl

The first thing I do on Thursday morning is call Cara. As soon as her momma gives her the phone, I say, "Can you skip swimming at the pool today? I need help me with my costume for the talent show."

"Sure. What kind of costume do you want?" she asks.

"I don't know," I admit. "All I know is I want a really good one!"

Cara giggles. Then she says, "Okay, tell me more when I get to your house. I'll come right over."

After we say goodbye and hang up, I head out to the front yard to wait for Cara. Ugly Brother waits too.

Before too long, Cara speeds up on her red racer bicycle.

We run inside and go upstairs to my bedroom. On the way up, I explain what I have in mind.

"I want something red, white, and blue, because I am singing a very patriotic song," I tell her.

"Do you have a white t-shirt and some red glitter?" she asks.

"Yes!" I say. The white shirt is in a drawer with my play clothes, so I pull it out.

While Cara waits, I dig around in my desk drawer for some red glitter.

She sits down on my bed. "Look for some glue, too, okay?" she says.

"Found it!" I shout, holding up the bottle of glue and the small jar of red glitter.

Cara spreads the t-shirt out on the floor so we can fix it up. She draws some stripes onto the shirt with a pencil.

I smear on the glue. Then Cara carefully shakes red glitter in between the pencil marks.

Ugly Brother wanders over to see what's going on. He tries to sniff my sparkly shirt. He gets the red glitter all over his nose.

"Don't you go sniffing glitter," I tell him. "Now you look like Rudolph the red-nosed reindeer!"

Cara and I laugh so hard we fall over on the floor. Ugly Brother is so silly!

Once we calm down, we put red glitter on my red flip-flops. There's glitter all over my room, sparkling on the floor.

Cara looks around and says, "With all this red glitter in your pink room, it looks like a Valentine's Day card."

"You're thinkin' about the wrong holiday! Remember, the Jubilee is a Fourth of July party," I reminder her.

Cara says, "I know, but I love pink and red together."

"What else should I wear?" I ask.

She thinks for a minute. Then she says, "It will be really hot outside. Are you gonna wear shorts?"

In the very bottom of one of my drawers, I find some blue shorts with white stars. "These will be perfect with my new sparkly top!" I exclaim.

"Do you want to borrow my headband with glittery blue stars on it?" Cara asks.

"Oh, yes! It will look so perfect with my costume," I reply.

Cara smiles. "You are going to be the only glitter girl in the talent show," she says.

I can't wait for the glue to dry so I can try on my glamorous glittery costume. But Cara can't wait to get back in the pool. She says, "I'm going to ride my bike over to the pool. Want to come?"

"Maybe later," I say. "But thanks for coming and helping me."

"You're welcome! See you later," she says. Then she waves and runs out of my room.

While I wait for the glue on my shirt and shoes to dry, I practice my song in front of my mirror. It is a tall oval mirror with a floor stand, and I can see all of me in it. I use a marker for a microphone. Then I sing my heart out.

I try to remember all the words and sing them nice and loud.

When I sing the song for the tenth time, Ugly Brother starts howling. I guess he's getting sick of my singing, but a singing queen needs her practice. I open my bedroom door and push him into the hall.

"Sorry, Ugly Brother," I say. "You better go downstairs if you don't want to listen to my beautiful singing anymore."

He doesn't argue or try to come back in my room. Instead he heads for the stairs. I slam my door and keep on singing.

After I sing the song about a hundred more times, I check my shirt. It is finally dry. Yippee!

I pull on my costume. Then I stand in front of my mirror.

Wow! I love my costume! When I get Cara's headband it will be perfect.

I race downstairs to show Momma and Ugly Brother. They are both in the kitchen.

"Look at my costume!" I exclaim.

Momma is surprised. "Wow!" she says. Then she asks, "Did you make it yourself?"

"Cara helped me make it," I say. "She's going to let me wear her blue headband with stars on it, too."

"That sounds perfect," Momma says.

Ugly Brother sniffs my leg.

Momma smiles. "Looks like Ugly Brother helped too," she says.

"How did you know?" I ask.

Momma points at Ugly Brother's nose. "His nose matches your costume," she says. Then she smiles again. "You and Cara are so creative. You're going to be a sparkly little star!"

Chapter Seven

Picnic Planning

On Friday morning, Momma and I get up bright and early. It's our job to plan the family Fourth of July picnic.

Momma wants to make a menu for our picnic lunch. "What should we have with our fried chicken?" she asks. "We have to have fried chicken or it won't seem like the Jubilee!"

"How about deviled eggs?" I suggest.

Ugly Brother agrees. "Ruff, ruff," he barks.

Ugly Brother really likes eggs, any way you cook them. On Saturday mornings he eats them scrambled and on Sundays he eats them fried. I think he would eat eggs every single day if Momma would make them for him.

I like eggs too, but I only like the yellow gooey part of the egg. The white part tastes like rubber. That seems gross to me.

"All right," Momma says. "It's hard to beat your granny's deviled eggs, so it's a good thing I have her recipe."

No one makes better deviled eggs than Granny! I even eat the white part when it's one of Granny's deviled eggs.

"What else?" Momma asks.

We think and talk and plan. Our menu continues to fill up. Momma writes down that we'll make potato salad, homemade pickles, biscuits, pies, and brownies.

Then an idea hits my brain like a crust on a cherry pie.

"We need something cold to drink," I tell Momma. "How about making pink lemonade?"

She says, "That's a great idea! I'll put it on the menu, along with a jug of sweet tea."

At last, our menu is finished. Time to start cooking!

Momma puts on her apron. It has big bright red cherries on it. I put on my pink apron with the cute little strawberries on it. You know pink is my color!

Then we get to work.

First, we have to boil the eggs.

Momma pulls a chair over to the counter. I climb up and stand on it, carefully putting all of the eggs in the pan. I count each one as I put them in the water. "One, two, three, four, five, six, seven, eight, nine, ten, eleven, twelve," I say.

When I get to twelve, Momma says, "You don't have to count them all. Just hurry and get them in the pan so we can put them on the burner."

It takes a long time for water to boil. Momma warned me a long time ago that if you watch a pot it won't boil. The sooner it boils, the sooner I can make the deviled eggs, so I don't look at the pot one single time. I don't even peek.

Instead, I squeeze lemons for the lemonade. You need muscles to be good at squeezing them. T.J. is a better lemon squeezer, but he is mowing the Parkers' lawn. He likes to mow early before it gets too hot outside.

As I'm squeezing lemons, the pan lid pops off of the egg pot and white foamy bubbles rush out all over the stove!

Ugly Brother runs all around the kitchen, barking.

"Oh no!" Momma shouts. She grabs some paper towels.

"Maybe we should've watched that pot after all," I say quietly. Momma laughs.

When she gets everything cleaned up, we put the boiled eggs into a bowl with ice water to cool them down.

Momma sighs. "Well, my dear, I think that was enough kitchen excitement for today," she says. "Don't you think?"

I am too busy peeling off the hard white shells to answer. That's my favorite part of making deviled eggs.

I roll the eggs back and forth on the kitchen table to crack them. Then I pull long white ribbons of shell off of each cooked egg.

"You're doing great," Momma says. "I count seven peeled eggs already, and that's not an easy job."

"Thanks, Momma," I say. Peeling eggs doesn't seem like something a beauty queen would do, but I like it. "I guess I could be an egg-peeling queen," I add.

Momma laughs. "You sure could," she says. "You'd be the best egg-peeling queen the world has ever seen."

While I finish peeling eggs, Momma rolls out pie dough for her cherry cheesecake pie. She hums along as I sing and scoop out the egg yolks.

When the crust is done, she adds the filling. She makes a thick layer of red cherries, then cheesecake filling, then more red cherries, and then more cheesecake filling.

"I love red and white stripe pie," I tell her.

"What a terrific name for my pie!" she exclaims. "From now on, that's what I'll call it. Red and White Stripe Pie."

I'm all done with the eggs. Momma's all done with the pie. But we have lots of things on our list! We have more to do.

"Can we make Daddy's favorite next?" I ask.

Momma says, "That's my plan."

Daddy's favorite is brownies. Momma gets started. She puts the cocoa, flour, eggs, sugar, and butter in a bowl.

"Can I please stir the brownies?" I ask.

Handing me a long wooden spoon, Momma says, "Yes, you can stir. Stirring is a good job for you." Then she adds, "When we're done, that dog better not have any chocolate on his face. Not everyone wants to share a spoon with him!"

Ugly Brother whines under the table. I feel so sorry for him. All morning, I have been nibbling tasty food. Momma does not like Ugly Brother to eat people food, but Daddy, T.J., and I are always sneaking him treats.

We pour the brownies into a big baking pan and slide them into the oven.

Then Momma and I start cleaning up the kitchen.

Somehow, a mysterious boiled egg winds up on the floor, making one happy doggie snack for Ugly Brother. He gobbles it down in one huge bite. Then he licks his lips in case he missed any.

Chapter Eight

4th of July Jubilee

When we get up on Saturday morning, it is hot enough to fry an egg on the sidewalk. After a quick breakfast of cold cereal we all start to get ready to go to the Jubilee.

Momma fries the chicken. The hot grease pops in the skillet as she drops the chicken pieces in. Daddy helps Momma by packing everything in our big brown picnic basket. T.J. finds the ice chest in the garage and loads it with ice. I get to carry the jug of sweet tea.

Once everything is ready, we all pile into the van. But as Daddy pulls out of the driveway, I notice that we forgot something important!

"Stop this van! Where's Ugly Brother?" I shout.

Daddy stops. I jump out. Ugly Brother is chasing the van. He's dragging the bag with my glitter girl outfit in it.

"Oh, Ugly Brother, you saved me! I really forgot two things!" I cry. Then I give him the biggest squeezy hug ever.

He wags his little tail. Then we all pile back into the van and we are off to Pecan Park for the fun.

It takes about fifteen minutes to get there. When we get to the park, I spy Pappy waving at us.

Pappy has a great spot picked out under a gigantic oak tree. It is the perfect shady spot. Daddy parks the van nearby so we can unload our picnic basket, blankets, and chairs.

Our spot is at the top of the hill. We can see everything! The playground, gazebo, craft tents, and lake are below us. I bet Granny is selling her jewelry in the craft tent.

Momma and Daddy are spreading out an old red-and-white striped quilt. Momma says, "Kylie Jean, run on down to the craft tent and tell Granny we'll come look when we get our picnic blanket set up."

I shrug. "Okay, Momma."

Then I run down the hill. When I get to the tent, it doesn't take me long to find Granny.

Lots of ladies are looking at her jewelry. Earrings, bracelets, and necklaces are spread out on a long table.

I sneak up behind Granny's table and give her a big hug.

I ask, "Did you sell the bracelet I made yet?"

She smiles. "I sold it right away!" she says. "It was a big hit."

"Momma says she'll come look once the picnic is set up," I report.

"I was just fixin' to head up there myself," Granny tells me. "Will you come with me?"

I nod. Granny sets a out a little sign that says "Be Back Soon." Then she takes my hand and we walk through the tent together. I peek at the other crafts as we walk through.

"Granny, I like some of this jewelry, but yours is the best," I say. "You make the prettiest bracelets in the whole wide world."

"Why, thank you, sugar," she says. A big smile hops onto her face.

Together, we walk up the hill. We get there just in time. Momma is unloading delicious food from the brown basket.

When she lifts out the big platter of deviled eggs, I squeal.

"Look, Granny!" I say. "I made your eggs! Momma helped me a little."

Granny smiles. "I have to say, I do make fantastic deviled eggs!" she says. "I bet yours are just as good."

Daddy laughs. "I hope you made extra, Kylie Jean," he says. "T.J. and I can eat a dozen all by ourselves."

I look around at all of the colorful quilts and picnic cloths spread out in the park around the big white gazebo. The picnics look like little happy islands of people. My best cousin, Lucy, is over by the creek with her momma and daddy and her big sister, Lilly. I wave at Lucy. She waves back at me.

Ugly Brother sits beside me, licking his nose. He smells that fried chicken.

"Not yet," I tell him. "We gotta wait till Momma is ready. How about I sing my song to you?"

He barks, "Ruff."

That means no. He is tired of hearing The Star-Spangled Banner.

Crossing my arms over my chest, I mutter, "I want you to know that even though you just hurt my feelings, I still love you. And I'm ready for the talent show anyway."

T.J. pats Ugly Brother. "You put up with a lot, so don't let her push you around," T.J. tells him.

Ugly Brother barks, "Ruff, ruff!"

Sometimes, my brothers gang up on me!

Finally, Momma says, "Let's eat!"

Granny and Pappy sit in their lawn chairs. Daddy makes a plate for Granny. I make one for Pappy. Daddy puts extra potato salad on Granny's plate. I put extra deviled eggs on Pappy's plate. First the plates are full. Then the stomachs are full.

We eat and eat and eat. Everything is so good. But then Momma asks, "Are y'all ready for our Red and White Stripe Pie?"

Everyone groans. We are all too full, except for Daddy. He says, "Where are those brownies?"

Momma passes him the plate. He takes three. "I always have room for brownies," he says, winking at me.

The grown-ups sit around, talking. After a while, T.J. goes to play Frisbee with his friends.

Lucky for me, Lucy runs over. "Come and play horseshoes with us," she says. "We're having lots of fun."

I say, "Okay." Lucy and I hold hands and run down the hill toward the creek, where our other cousins are throwing horseshoes.

The horseshoes are heavy. We have to throw them at a stake that's stuck in the ground. Our big cousins can toss them real easily, but I have to throw them with two hands. So does Lucy. We both miss a lot, but we're having fun.

Clang, clang, clang go the horseshoes. But I keep thinking about singing my song for the talent show in the big white gazebo.

Chapter Nine
Talent Show Time

Before long, I see Momma walking over to us. She calls, "Kylie Jean, it's time to get ready!"

It's almost talent show time!

As we walk away from the horseshoes, Lucy yells, "Good luck, Kylie Jean!" I turn around and wave at her.

I see that Momma is carrying the bag with my glitter girl outfit in it. "Where am I gonna change?" I ask nervously.

"Don't worry," Momma says. "I have a plan."

I follow her to the park restrooms. But inside, I see that Momma wasn't the only one with this plan! There are girls and ladies everywhere. They are changing, putting on makeup, and fixing their hair. I see some square dancers. Their slips are really fluffy.

"Where can I change?" I ask Momma.

Pointing to a tiny open spot in the corner, Momma asks, "How about right there?"

We weave through the twirler girls with their batons, more square dancers, and past a girl with a big silver guitar.

Finally, I can see my changing spot. Momma hands over my bag. I pull everything out.

While I put on my costume, she tries to fix my hair, brushing out all the tangles. Then she hands me the headband with the stars that Cara let me borrow. It is just perfect.

At last, I'm ready.

I am wearing my glitter girl red and white striped shirt, my shorts, my glittery flip-flops, and Cara's headband. I kind of look like the flag!

Someone shouts, "Five minutes before we have to line up!"

Momma winks at me.

"We better go line up since you're all ready," she says.

We cross the park to the gazebo. Behind it is a table where the performers sign in. In front of the gazebo is the stage.

I step up to the table. "My name is Kylie Jean Carter and I'm a singer in the show," I say.

The girl working the table gives me a card with the number twenty-three on it. That's a really big number! I ask, "How many numbers are there for this talent show?"

She says, "Twenty-four. You are right before the last performer. We went by the order y'all signed up in. Did you sign up late?"

I reply, "Yes, ma'am."

I wish my number was fifteen. Fifteen is one of my luckiest numbers. My birthday is on the 15th. I like five, too, since there are five people in my family. Number twenty-three means I will have to wait a long, long time for my turn.

"Don't worry," Momma whispers. "You'll be busy watching the show. It'll be your turn before you know it." I nod. Momma is right.

I can't take my eyes off of the performer who is going to go first. He is warming up by juggling a plate, a cup, three balls, and some red, white, and blue rings. Pointing in his direction, I say, "He's good!"

Momma waits with me in line. The talent show is about to start and everyone in the park moves closer to the gazebo. That's when I start to get nervous!

Chapter Ten

Showtime!

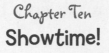

I listen to the mayor of our town, Mr. Richardson, announce the performers.

He calls out, "Let's get this show started! Everyone, give a big hand for our first performer, Dan the Juggling Man."

I watch Dan juggle some more. He is awesome! Next, several dance groups perform. I watch tap dancers and square dancers. One of the square dancers has on a pink and white dress with a big fluffy pink slip.

I whisper, "I want to learn how to square dance."

Momma whispers back, "You just want a pink dress like that dancer has on!"

I laugh, covering my mouth. Momma sure does know me!

The magician's act is really interesting until his rabbit gets stuck in his hat. Someone in line says he should have practiced more.

He's a kid, just like me.

Lots of people cheer for the baton twirlers. They have plain batons, not the kind you light on fire.

The fiery batons would be more exciting. They are number fifteen.

I whisper to Momma, "I wish I was number fifteen, because I sure do like that number, and if I was number fifteen I'd be all done now."

Momma smiles and pats my shoulder. "It won't be long now," she says.

Number sixteen is a bunch of little girls doing gymnastics. They take lessons at Tammy's Tumbling School. They get mixed up and bump into each other.

One of them starts to cry, and her momma has to go get her off the stage in front of everyone!

Then there are more singers. A church group sings. After that, we watch more dancers.

Then there's an old man with a puppet in his lap. The puppet talks.

That doesn't make a lot of sense to me, so I ask Momma quietly, "Momma, how does the puppet talk?"

Momma says, "The puppet is called a dummy, because it can't talk. The man is doing the talking, but it sounds like it's coming from the dummy."

Finally, it's my turn. I'm nervous. I feel like I swallowed a bowl full of June bugs!

Mr. Richardson says, "Folks, up next is Kylie Jean Carter, singin' The Star-Spangled Banner."

Everyone claps as I walk to the center of the stage. I stand right in front of the microphone and then I start to sing as loud as I can.

I'm glad I practiced my song a lot. The words are easy for me now.

On my third time through, I say, "Come on, y'all! You know the song. Sing it with me!"

Everyone starts to sing. I see Lucy and Cara singing. Daddy, Granny, and everybody in my family — they're all singing too.

At the end, I tell everyone, "I just love America, so Happy Birthday to the good ole USA."

I'm pretty sure I'm gonna win it.

Then Mandy Howard comes up to sing. She's number twenty-four. She sings so pretty my heart wants to float right out of my chest. I never heard a singer with a voice as sweet as hers! That's when I realize I want Mandy to win. She deserves it.

When the judges announce the winners, third place goes to Dan the Juggling Man.

Mr. Richardson calls my name for second place. I jump up and down. Momma gives me a big squeezy hug. I look for Daddy, T.J., and Ugly Brother, but I can't see them.

Then Mr. Richardson calls out, "First place, Mandy Howard."

I shout, "Yes!"

And even though I didn't win, I am as happy as butter on a biscuit.

Chapter Eleven
Fireworks, Sparklers, and Singers

My family expects me to be sad, but I'm not sad at all. I'm glad Mandy won. She deserved it the most! Her voice was just so pretty!

"Good for you," Daddy says. "You did a wonderful job and you're not a sore loser."

"You're not a loser at all," T.J. says. He even gives me a hug!

When the sky is finally the color of black ink, the real show begins.

You know I just love the fireworks!

All around the park, sparklers blink like fireflies. About a million people are waiting for the fireworks to start. Some sit on quilts, others on the fronts of their cars.

Mr. Richardson and Mandy find me lying on my blanket in the field.

"How about a song from our Jubilee talent show winners while we wait for the fireworks to start?" Mr. Richardson asks. "You and Mandy would do a lovely duet."

That sounds so fun! I like the idea of singing again!

I look at Momma. "Can I do it?" I ask. "I really want to."

"Go ahead," Momma says. "We'll be right here."

"Okay," I say. I follow Mandy over to the piano in the gazebo.

She whispers, "Sit beside me. We'll sing America the Beautiful. You sing the America, America part. Okay?"

I wiggle with excitement. "Yup, I got it," I whisper back. Then Mandy starts to play the song and we sing.

Suddenly, it seems like a thousand voices are singing with us. Everyone in town knows the words to our song, and everyone wants to sing along. The voices blend, making a giant choir singing in the night.

Above us, the night sky explodes with electric color. The fireworks light up the gazebo as we finish our song.

Mandy and I stand together. The crowd is clapping so loud it sounds like thunder.

Mandy blows kisses. I do my beauty queen wave, nice and slow, side to side.

Even a second-place singer can sparkle like a real, true beauty queen!

Kylie Jean

Drama Queen

Table of Contents

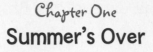

Chapter One
Summer's Over

On Sunday afternoon, right at the tail end of summer, Momma, Daddy, T.J., and I are all visiting Lickskillet Farm, where Nanny and Pa live. Everybody in my whole family is at the farm for Sunday dinner.

T.J. and the boys are out in the pasture. The grown-ups are talking while they sit in the yard and drink lemonade. The big girls are inside, gossiping.

Everyone is here except Ugly Brother. He had to stay at home.

Me and my best cousin, Lucy, are sitting on the fence. Lucy is exactly the same age as me.

My face is covered up by a big ole slice of sweet pink watermelon. Pink is my most favorite color.

Lucy looks at me and laughs.

"What's so funny?" I ask.

"You've been eating that melon right straight down the middle. It looks like a heart," she says. "Plus, there's pink juice drippin' off your chin."

"Watermelon only tastes good when it's messy," I say. Then I whisper, "I just love spittin' the seeds out, too. Don't you tell anyone. That is not how beauty queens act."

I spit out three little black seeds. They fly like little black bugs and land one by one in the pasture. Plop, plop, plop.

Lucy crosses her heart. "I promise to never ever tell that Kylie Jean Carter is a seed-spitter," she says.

We both spit out more seeds. They shoot into the pasture and land in little black piles.

Our dusty legs swing over the rail as we sit and spit. I smile up at the hot sun as it kisses all of my little brown freckles.

It is a good day for the last day of summer.

Tomorrow is the first day of school, but we have the rest of the afternoon to play at the farm.

After Lucy and I finish our watermelon, we run through the tall gold grass into the mud next to the pond. I can feel it squishing between my toes. Then we slip our dirty bare feet into the warm blue water. The pond smells good, like rain.

When it is almost dark, the mosquitoes start to bite, and Lucy keeps slapping her legs.

"We better go on in," Lucy says. "It's time for supper."

We walk toward the tiny white farmhouse right in the middle of a hot pink watermelon sky. Black birds fly by like little black seeds.

Summer is almost gone, and the sun is going away, too. It is a shimmering orange ball floating lazily near the ground. Lightning bugs start to flicker in the grass. Today is almost over.

Tomorrow will be a big adventure. My heart starts to pound. Tomorrow, I will be in a whole new grade at Lee Elementary School.

Chapter Two
A New Teacher

I don't sleep one little itty-bitty teeny tiny wink that night. No sir. Going to second grade is too exciting!

On Monday morning, I sit up in my bed and look around my room. I see my new pink backpack with hearts on it. Then I see my new pink sneakers with silver laces. After that, I see my pile of school supplies. My pink pencil box is full of pencils, a glue stick, erasers, crayons, and markers. I am ready!

I hop out of bed and get dressed. I picked out my outfit last night, so it is all ready for me.

I put on my blue skirt with the ruffles, my new pink top, and my tiara.

"T.J. and Kylie Jean," Momma calls, "come and get your breakfast. You're going to be late on your first day if you don't hurry up!"

I rush downstairs to the big sunny kitchen. Momma made pancakes and bacon for us to eat. T.J.'s pancakes are normal, but Momma made mine so they look like hearts.

T.J. is already eating when I sit down. "You better hurry up," he says with his mouth full. "You know Mr. Jim won't wait for us if you're late."

Mr. Jim is the man who drives our school bus. Some kids think he's mean, but I like him.

Ugly Brother comes to the table too. He sits down next to me and looks at me with his big brown eyes.

"You just have to eat some of this tasty bacon," I tell him. Under the table, I feed him three pieces of bacon. Ugly Brother gobbles them up. Then he licks my fingers real good.

"Do you like bacon?" I ask him.

"Ruff, ruff," he replies.

Two barks mean yes. One bark means no. He likes it!

"Come on, Kylie Jean," T.J. says. "Quit feedin' the dog. We have to go."

I run to the kitchen sink and wash my hands good. Then I'm ready to go!

My backpack is loaded up with school supplies. When I swing it on to my back I nearly topple right over.

My big brother is getting awful bossy now. He just grabs my hand and drags me to the front door. In his other hand, he is holding my new lunch box with red hearts on the front. "Come on, now," he tells me.

"Bye, Ugly Brother. Bye, Momma. Love you, " I shout. T.J. slams the door behind us.

The big yellow bus full of new faces pulls up right in front of our house. Mr. Jim opens the bus door. T.J. has to push me up the steps because my backpack is so heavy.

Mr. Jim waves us to the back of the bus. It's hot and smells like Cheetos in here.

The bus is crowded, so T.J. and I have to squeeze in a seat with one of his friends.

First, the bus pulls up in front of the high school. "See ya later, Lil' Bit," T.J. tells me. When he and his friend are gone, I have more room. I scoot over to the window and watch T.J. walk into the high school. Then Mr. Jim drives away.

Before long, Mr. Jim parks the bus in front of Robert E. Lee Elementary School. The bus door opens and kids roll out like shiny new marbles. I get pushed along with the crowd, out of the bus, up the sidewalk, and into the building.

Inside the school, all the kids are looking for their new classrooms. Momma told me just where to go. I head straight to Room 101.

My new teacher is standing in the doorway. She is very beautiful. Her hair is brown, darker than mine, and her dress is bright blue with big hot pink flowers on it. I like her already! All teachers should wear something pink.

"Hello," she says, smiling at me. "I like your tiara! Go on in, choose a desk, and find the cubby with your name on it."

"All right," I tell her, smiling back.

Inside Room 101, the desks are pushed together to make little squares. Each square is made up of four desks.

There is a row of cubbies against one of the sky-blue walls. I find my name on one of them and put my backpack in my new cubby.

"Hey, Kylie Jean!" someone says. I look and see my friend Cara sitting nearby. I sit right down next to her.

"Is Lucy here yet?" I ask. Cara shakes her head. I gasp. "Late to school on the first day?" I whisper. That's not like Lucy!

Then an idea hits my brain like mud on a noonday pig. I'm going to save Lucy a desk! The one right across from me will do just fine.

But before I can put my new pink pencil box on that desk, a tall new girl sits down right in the spot I want for Lucy.

"I'm new," she says. "My name is Paula. But you may call me Miss Paula Dupree." Then she holds her hand out to shake mine.

I do not like her already! She just walked right over and stole Lucy's spot!

I don't shake her hand. "Then you may call me Your Majesty," I say, pointing at my tiara. I add, "And you may be Miss Paula Dupree, but you're sittin' in my cousin Lucy's spot. Please move!"

Paula glares at me. She looks down at the desk and then back up. "I don't see her name on it, so it's mine now," she says.

"You could move over one seat," Cara says.

"No, I could not," Paula tells her. "The teacher said to choose a desk, and I chose this one. This is a free country and we don't have a queen," she adds, looking right at my tiara. "And besides, I was here first."

"Please?" I ask nicely.

Paula shakes her head. "No way," she says. She crosses her arms and rolls her eyes at me.

I'm too mad to say anything. I just walk over and put my pink pencil box on the desk across from Cara. I guess my best cousin won't get to sit across from me.

"I'll trade with you, Kylie Jean," Cara offers. "Then you can sit across from Lucy."

"Oh, thank you!" I say. "That is so kind!" I narrow my eyes at Paula. She looks away.

Finally, Lucy runs into the room. I wave at her and point at my pink pencil box.

"Sit here!" I say.

Lucy puts her backpack in the cubby with her name on it. Then she sits down across from me and looks at Paula. "Are you new?" Lucy asks Paula.

"I am indeed. You may call me Miss Paula Dupree," Paula says. Then she sticks her nose up in the air. She is really bugging me, this new girl! I don't think I like her!

Lucy laughs. "I think I'll call you Paula," she says. "What you said is too long, and I'm sure I'll forget it." She winks at me. My cousin can tell from looking at me that I'm mad enough to spit nails!

Just then, the bell rings, and our teacher closes the door. She walks up to the board. Her pretty dress swishes as she walks. On the board, she writes, "My name is Ms. Corazón."

Our new teacher looks at the students in Room 101.

"Good morning, students!" she says. "Welcome to second grade. I have planned so many fun things for us to do this year. We will take trips, do experiments, and even put on a class play. I just know you'll love second grade!"

We all smile at her, even Paula.
"First I will take attendance,"
Ms. Corazón says, "and
then we will start with
today's lessons."

She picks up a piece of
paper and starts calling out
names.

The names are in ABC order.
Alice, Cara, Danny, Eva,
Greg, Hanna, Jessie, Kylie.

When she calls my name, I say, "Here!" and
raise my hand.

Ms. Corazón sees my raised hand and frowns.
She asks, "Kylie, is something wrong?"

I nod. "My real name is Kylie Jean," I say. "I have two parts to my name."

Ms. Corazón smiles. She picks up a pencil and writes on her paper. "Okay, Kylie Jean," she says. "I made a note on my attendance sheet. I won't forget the second part of your name again!"

She continues calling names. Lucy, Mark, Nico, Paula. Paula raises her hand and waves it in the air like a chicken flapping its wings.

"Yes, Paula?" Ms. Corazón asks.

Paula stands up. "My name is Miss Paula Dupree," she says loudly. "Please change it on your paper."

Ms. Corazón raises her eyebrows. Then she frowns. "Paula, you're still a young lady," she says. "I'll just call you Paula."

This makes Paula mad! She crosses her arms and her eyes look as dark as thunder clouds. She looks over at me and sticks out her tongue.

Beauty queens do not stick out their tongues. Ignoring her is the best plan. I just keep my eyes on Ms. Corazón. I can tell already she's going to be the best teacher ever!

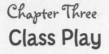

Chapter Three
Class Play

All morning, we work on reading. Then we go to art class. My friends and I ignore Paula as best as we can, but it's awful hard. The first thing she does in art class is complain about the aprons we have to wear. She says they smell bad. Well, they do, but she doesn't have to be a baby about it!

When we get back to Room 101, Ms. Corazón waits until we're all sitting down. Then she says, "It's time for lunch, but first, I have something very exciting to tell you."

We all wait.

Ms. Corazón goes on, "We'll be doing *Alice in Wonderland* for our class play! I know y'all will love it."

A lot of kids raise their hands to ask questions, but Ms. Corazón shakes her head. "Time for lunch," she says. "We can talk more about the play later. Please line up at the door."

My friends and I sit together in the cafeteria. We all brought our lunches from home. Paula gets in line for hot lunch. Then she stands in the front of the cafeteria, looking for a place to sit.

It must be real hard to be the new girl.

I get up and run over to her. "Come on, Paula," I say. "You can sit with us." She doesn't look sure, but she follows me back to our table anyway.

Just like Momma says, pretty is as pretty does. I know I have to try to be nice to Paula, even if she's mean.

Paula puts her tray on the table right next to my lunchbox. Then she plops down in her chair. She looks at my lunchbox.

"I don't bring my lunch," she tells us. "My parents aren't poor, so I can buy my lunch at school."

It takes all my strength to hold my tongue!

I take my sandwich, chips, apple slices, and chocolate chip cookies out of my red heart lunchbox.

There's a folded-up piece of paper in the bottom. I open it up.

Kylie Jean,

Have a great
first day at
school.
Love,
Momma

X O X O X O

Paula grabs my note. She reads it, laughs, and wads it up into a ball. "You must be a big baby if your mom has to put notes in your lunch to keep you from crying at school," she says. "Do you miss your mama, Kylie Jean? Boo hoo, you big baby!"

Now I'm really mad. I open my mouth to say something, but Cara does first.

"Paula, Kylie Jean isn't a baby. Her mom just does that to be nice. And we can buy our lunch, but we don't because school lunch tastes super gross," Cara says.

"That's true," I say. I look at Paula's lunch. It looks pretty gross. The lettuce is brown and the pepperoni pizza is all mushy. I would never want to eat it!

I repeat to myself, *Pretty is as pretty does.*

Then I look at Paula. "I know you made fun of my lunch," I say, "but I'll give you half of my turkey sandwich. Do you want it?"

Paula looks at the greasy pizza and brown salad on her tray. Then she shrugs and reaches for half of my sandwich. She eats it in two bites.

"I think *Alice in Wonderland* is perfect for our class play. Don't you?" I ask my friends.

Lucy laughs. "You just want to be the Queen of Hearts," she says.

"Yep!" I say. I sure do want to be the Queen. "If I am, I'll get to wear a real crown," I add, pointing to the sparkly tiara on my head.

Paula rolls her eyes. "Your tiara is dumb," she says. "And it's not real."

"Hush your mouth, Paula," Cara tells her. "Quit pickin' on Kylie Jean."

Paula gets up. "I don't want to sit with a bunch of babies," she tells us.

She picks up her tray and storms away.

My friends and I look at each other. "I'm glad she's gone," I whisper.

"She's mean," Lucy says.

I nod.

"We're not babies," Cara says.

I nod.

But I can tell from my friends' faces that they feel just as bad as I do.

Chapter Four
Getting Ready
for Wonderland

After recess, I stop to get a drink of water. When I'm done, Paula is standing in the doorway of Room 101. She steps in front of me when I try to walk through the door.

I move to the right, but she moves too! Then I move to the left, and she steps right in front of me again!

Finally, I push past her.

Lucy and Cara are waiting at our desks. "Did she try to keep you out?" Cara asks. "We should start calling her Paula DuMEAN!"

I frown. I don't know for sure if Cara is right. Name-calling is mean, too, and beauty queens aren't mean.

"Momma always says you have to act pretty to be pretty," I say quietly.

I look over at Paula. She's still standing in the doorway. Now she's trying to block Hanna from coming into our room. Hanna is real little, and she looks like she might cry.

"Paula's mean," Cara tells me. "If she's mean, we can be mean back."

Ms. Corazón walks up to the door. "Please find your seat, girls," she says to Paula and Hanna, smiling.

Paula quickly runs to her desk and sits down. Hanna slowly walks to her seat.

"Let's get started with *Alice in Wonderland*!" Ms. Corazón says.

She's carrying a stack of booklets. She walks around the room, handing one booklet to each student.

"On Friday, we'll have tryouts for all of the parts," Ms. Corazón tells us. "There are sixteen parts in the play."

I look around the room. There are more than sixteen kids in my class. But Ms. Corazón sees my worried look and adds, "Some people won't be in the play. That's okay, because we need some kids to help move things around on the stage. They're called stagehands, and they work behind the scenes."

Being a stagehand is not for me. I'm only going to practice the part of the Queen of Hearts.

Right from the very beginning, I knew it was the part for me! She's not a beauty queen, but she gets to wear a crown.

I open the booklet to page one. I need to get down to business. By Friday, I want to know all of the words without looking at the paper.

Chapter 5
After School

The day seems to drag on for hours. When the three o'clock bell finally rings, I run out of Room 101. I don't stop running until I get out to the bus and hop on. I'm the very first person on the bus!

"What's your hurry?" Mr. Jim asks. "Bad day at school?"

I shake my head. "No sir," I tell him. "I just need to get home real quick."

Mr. Jim smiles. "Well, it might be a minute," he says. "You have to wait for all the other kids, and then we have to pick up the high school kids."

I sigh. This might take longer than I thought! "All right," I say. I down sit in the first seat in the front row. That way I can get off the bus faster. Then I have to wait and wait some more. Soon all of the kids from Lee Elementary are on the bus. Mr. Jim nods at me. Then we take off for the high school.

T.J. is the last high school kid on the bus. "Hey, Lil' Bit," he says, sitting down next to me.

I'm mad at him for taking so long, so I decide not to talk to him all the way home! I just turn away and stare out the window.

"What did I do?"

T.J. asks. When I don't answer, he just sighs. "Whatever, Kylie Jean," he grumbles.

When we get to our house on Peachtree Lane, I fly off the bus and zoom straight for the front door. T.J. walks slower and comes in after me.

I holler, "Ugly Brother!" and run through the living room to the kitchen.

Momma is in the kitchen, making us an afternoon snack. I sit down at the table and call for Ugly Brother again.

"Ugly Brother is at the vet with your daddy," Momma says. "Remember? He's getting his shots today."

That makes me feel terrible! My poor Ugly Brother. I put my head in my hands.

Momma smiles a nice smile. She can tell I feel bad.

She slides a plate of warm brownies in front of me. She used a cookie cutter to make them into hearts!

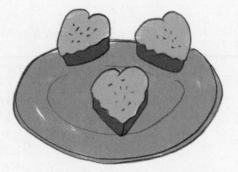

"Why don't you tell me all about your first day at school, sugar?" Momma asks. "Was it good?"

I shrug and stuff a brownie in my mouth. "Parf of if wath goob," I tell her. Then I swallow and try again. "Part of it was good," I say. "But part of it was bad."

"What was bad?" Momma asks.

"There's a new girl," I tell her. I fill her in on Paula.

Momma frowns. "I don't like the idea of someone calling you a baby," she says. "But I think you made too big of a deal about the desk for Lucy. Paula didn't steal Lucy's seat. Ms. Corazón said you could all choose your seats. And Lucy was the one who was late to school!"

I nod. "I know, Momma," I say. "But then I tried to be nice, and Paula was real mean."

Momma shakes her head. "Pretty is as pretty does," she says. "What else happened today? What was the good part?"

I start telling Momma what stagehands are, but she already knows. So we talk about the play. I tell her about all the different parts.

"Let me guess," Momma says. "You want to be Alice."

"No way, Momma!" I say. "First of all, Alice has 125 lines, so Ms. Corazón says four girls have to play Alice. I want to be the only one playing my part."

"What part is that?" Momma asks.

"The Queen of Hearts!" I say. "Of course."

"And how many lines does the Queen of Hearts have?" Momma asks, reaching over to straighten my tiara.

"Thirty-two," I tell her. "I already memorized two. That means I only have thirty left to go, and then I'll know them all! But how can I learn all the lines?"

"Copy them down over and over again," Momma says. "When I was in plays in college, that always helped me."

"Momma!" I whisper, shocked. "I never knew you were a famous actress!"

Momma laughs. "I wasn't famous, Kylie Jean," she says. Then she winks and adds, "There's a lot you don't know about your momma! Now finish your snack and run upstairs to practice."

I finish up the crumbs of brownies and head upstairs. I find a pretty pencil with a heart-shaped eraser and a pad of paper with pink hearts on it. They will help me get in the mood to be the Queen.

I start copying the Queen of Hearts's lines from the play book Ms. Corazón passed out. But after I write about ten lines down, my hand starts to hurt. Then I hear the front door close.

"Ugly Brother!" I shout.

I run downstairs. My poor dog is standing there, with his tail down. He's walking slow and looks real sad.

I bend down next to him. "Did it hurt?" I whisper, putting my arms around him.

"Ruff, ruff," he barks quietly. That means yes. Poor Ugly Brother.

I stand up. "I have just the thing to make you feel better," I tell him. "Come on!"

When Ugly Brother sees that I'm walking into the kitchen, his ears perk up and he slowly follows me.

First I find the stepstool. Then I take down two bowls from the cupboard and find some vanilla ice cream in the freezer.

Momma walks in as I'm scooping ice cream into the bowls. "What are you doing, Kylie Jean?" she asks.

"Making Ugly Brother feel better," I tell her.

"Who's the other bowl for?" Momma asks.

"Me, of course!" I say.

"Oh, Kylie Jean," Momma says. She smiles. "Sometimes I don't know what to do with you."

Chapter Six
Tryouts

After school on Tuesday, I know I need to get down to business. I only have three days left till the tryouts, and I only have five lines memorized.

First things first, I need to look like the Queen of Hearts. In my closet, I find the Little Red Riding Hood cape I wore for Halloween last year.

I put it on and look in the mirror. Close, but not close enough.

I find some white socks and pins in Momma's room. I pin the socks around the edge of my cape, so it looks like a fur trim.

Next, I cut out a giant red heart from some paper in my room. I glue glitter all over it. You can't be a queen without some sparkle! I pin the heart to the back of my cape. Then I add a gold crown.

I look in the mirror. I think I look great, but I need a second opinion. "Ugly Brother!" I yell. He comes running into the room. "How do I look?" I ask. "Do I look right for the part?"

He barks, "Ruff, ruff!"

Two barks! That means yes!

I decide I'll wear the outfit all week whenever I'm at home. That way, by Friday, I'll be ready. Momma says this is called getting into character.

In the morning, I practice while we eat.

Momma sets the breakfast table with a pretty
teapot so I can practice pouring the tea.

"More tea?" I ask the
White Rabbit.

Ugly Brother says,
"Ruff, ruff!"

He's pretty good as the White Rabbit. He knows
the character.

After school, we practice in the back yard.

"Off with their heads!" I yell.

That part scares Ugly Brother, so he puts his
paws over his eyes.

At bedtime, we practice too. I shout, "Bring me
the Duchess!"

Ugly Brother brings me a Barbie. For practice, Barbie makes an okay Duchess.

By Friday morning, I'm ready. That's good, because T.J. is really sick of me practicing. "Off with your head, Kylie Jean!" he says when I come down to breakfast. "I'm so sick of the Queen of Hearts! I can even hear you in my sleep."

"Stop it, T.J.," Momma says. "How did you sleep, Kylie Jean? Are you ready for your big day?"

"Yes ma'am," I tell her. "I sure am!"

"Where's your costume?" Daddy asks.

"I don't need it today," I announce. I shake my hair. I'm wearing my sparkly red heart barrettes. "These barrettes will show that I am the true Queen of Hearts," I explain.

Daddy stands up. "I better get to work," he says. "Break a leg, honey."

I frown. "Daddy, are you being mean to me?" I ask quietly.

Daddy smiles. "That's show-biz talk," he explains. "It means good luck."

"Oh!" I say. "Thanks, Daddy."

I start to get nervous on the bus. "Calm down, Lil' Bit," T.J. says before he gets off at the high school. "You'll be great. I bet nobody practiced near as much as you did."

When the bus stops at Lee Elementary School, I go straight to Room 101. Ms. Corazón is at the door waiting to greet us. She says, "Good morning, Kylie Jean! I like your barrettes."

Cara and Lucy are waiting for me at our desks. I smile and wave, nice and slow, side to side, like a true beauty queen. "Good morning!" I say.

Then I hear a loud voice coming from the classroom door. I turn around and my mouth falls right open.

Paula Dupree is standing in the door. She's wearing a Queen of Hearts costume. She looks just like the queen in the movie, and I know, because I watched it ten times this week.

Cara whispers, "Do you two see Paula DuMean?"

Lucy nods. Then she says, "Don't worry, Kylie Jean. You'll be so good, no one will notice her fancy costume. You have on your pretty red heart barrettes."

Tears come to my eyes. I worked so hard, and now I don't have the right clothes to be Queen.

Lucy whispers, "Queens don't cry in front of people, Kylie Jean."

I nod. She's right. Queens aren't babies. I take a deep breath and smile.

Later, we all read our parts for Ms. Corazón. I'm the only person who doesn't have to read from the play book, because I know all my lines by heart.

I make my voice loud when the Queen is mad and quiet when she is thinking.

Just like I thought, Paula wants to be the Queen of Hearts, too. But she has to read all her lines.

When she's done, I say, "You did a good job."

I think Paula will tell me I did a good job, too, but she just says, "I know."

Ms. Corazón says, "It's going to be very hard to choose just one of you to be the Queen of Hearts."

I smile at her and turn my head so she'll notice my heart barrettes. Ms. Corazón winks at me. Then she says, "Everyone who tried out will get a part. I'll tell you all on Monday!"

I can hardly wait. I just know she's going to pick me!

Chapter Seven
Cast Assignments

Luckily, the weekend goes real fast, and before I know it, it's Monday morning!

Today, T.J. doesn't have to bug me. I get ready and eat my breakfast lickety-split. I run out the door and am waiting for the bus ten minutes before it's supposed to get there.

When I finally get to school, a bunch of kids are standing in front of Room 101. I am too short to see, so I keep jumping up and down trying to see over them.

Cara is close to the front, reading the paper on the door. She pushes her way out. Then she sees me.

"Did I get the part of the Queen?" I ask.

"Well, you did get a part," Cara replies, looking down at the ground.

"The Queen?" I ask again.

She shakes her head. "Alice!" she tells me.

That can't be right. I don't even have yellow hair like Alice does! Maybe it's a mistake. It's just a bad dream. Maybe I'm asleep and still dreaming.

"Cara, pinch me, quick!" I beg.

Cara reaches over and pinches me. Hard. Too hard!

"OUCH!" I shout.

"Sorry," Cara says. "Come on, let's go sit down."

I follow her to our desks. Paula is already sitting down. She says, "Congratulations, Alice. You know, you have the star role, but I get to play the Queen. It's the perfect part for me. I love giving orders."

I can't believe my ears. Paula DuMean gets to be the Queen! How could Ms. Corazón give her the part? Paula didn't even know all her lines. I did. Why can't I be the Queen?

As soon as Ms. Corazón walks in, I run over to her quick as I can. "How are you today, Kylie Jean?" she asks, smiling at me as she puts a stack of papers on her desk.

"Well, to be honest, ma'am, I'm not so good," I tell her.

Ms. Corazón frowns. "What's the matter?" she asks.

I sigh. "I think you must have made a mistake when you did the parts for the play," I explain. "I'm the one who's supposed to be the Queen. Paula didn't even know her lines! And did you forget that I have brown hair? Alice has yellow hair."

"I know you have brown hair," Ms. Corazón says. She grins at me. "I have a surprise for you!" She reaches into one of her desk drawers and pulls out a big, floppy blond wig.

"You'll get to wear this during the play," Ms. Corazón says.

"But I still think I should be the Queen of Hearts," I tell her. I don't want to touch the wig. It looks weird. She lets it fall onto her desk.

"Kylie Jean, I gave the role of Alice to the girls who did the best job memorizing their lines," Ms. Corazón tells me. She smiles. "And you were the very best at memorizing!"

"But I didn't want to be Alice," I tell her. I feel tears stinging my eyes like little bees. "I wanted to be the Queen."

Ms. Corazón nods. She pats my hand. "I understand," she says. "But Paula is going to be the Queen."

She looks at me for a moment. Then she adds, "I'll tell you what. If Paula gets sick, or can't be the Queen, you can be her understudy."

When she sees my confused look, she explains, "That's the person who steps in if an actor can't perform."

"Okay," I say sadly. "I guess that's better than nothin'." But I know it's not. I'm doomed to play Alice while Paula DuMean gets the role of the Queen of Hearts.

For the rest of the day, I feel worse than a dog on a short leash.

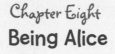

Chapter Eight
Being Alice

When I get home from school, I'm still feeling lower than a doodle bug. I don't want to eat the peanut butter and apple snack Momma makes for me. I don't want to play with Ugly Brother. I don't want to do anything.

But I know I have to put a smile on my face and try. I can't just up and quit, so I have to learn Alice's lines.

Ugly Brother walks over and sits down next to the kitchen table. He rests his head on my feet because he can tell I'm sad.

"You did a good job of helping me with being the Queen," I tell Ugly Brother. He looks up at me with his big brown eyes. I reach down and pat him. "But we have to start over after all our hard work," I say. "I'm going to be Alice. Will you please help me again?"

He replies, "Ruff, ruff!"

I pull the yellow wig from my backpack and put it on. Ugly Brother goes crazy barking. Then he runs out of the kitchen and into the living room. He hides behind the couch.

"Silly!" I shout, getting up to follow him. "It's me, Kylie Jean! Your sister!" I peek over the back of the couch.

"Ruff!" Ugly Brother barks.

Momma walks in to see what all the hollering is about. "Maybe you should practice without the wig," she suggests.

I take it off. Then Ugly Brother comes over and jumps up on me like I've been gone away on vacation or something. He licks my face. "Let's get to work," I tell him.

Alice talks to everyone, so now Ugly Brother has to be lots of different people. Sometimes he gets confused and doesn't know who he's supposed to be. I'm Alice Number 1, so all of my lines are in the beginning of the play.

Some kids didn't get parts with lines. They'll be mushrooms or flowers. I know I'm lucky, but I still wish I could be the Queen.

Chapter Nine
Practice Makes Perfect

Lucy, Cara, Sophie, and I are the four Alices. Sophie has to wear the wig too. Her real hair is red. All the Alices have to share a costume. That's okay, except Cara is tall. When she wears the costume the skirt is kind of short.

On Tuesday, we practice the play after lunch. I'm trying to be the best Alice I can.

I'm glad that I don't have to be Alice when Paula is playing the Queen of Hearts. That would make me too sad. But Cara is the Alice in that scene.

My part is fun. I get to play Alice when she is getting big and small. When she's big, I stand on a box. When she's small, I crouch down.

After practice, Ms. Corazón tells me I'm doing a wonderful job. "Who helps you practice?" she asks. "Your mother?"

"Nope," I tell her. "Ugly Brother helps me most of the time."

Ms. Corazón frowns. "You shouldn't call your brother names," she says. "What's his real name?"

"His name is Bruno," I say. "But everybody calls him Ugly Brother. Even Momma!"

Ms. Corazón shakes her head. "That poor boy," she says sadly.

"He's fine, ma'am," I say. "He did have shots last week, but he's okay now. I've been giving him doggy treats and ice cream whenever he helps me!"

Now she looks shocked. I head back over to my desk and sit down. "I don't know why Ms. Corazón is so worried about my dog!" I whisper to Lucy.

Lucy shrugs. "Maybe you've been giving him too much ice cream," she says.

Chapter 10
Red Spots

On Wednesday morning, we start to paint the set for our play. The set is the decorations that will go up behind us so the audience knows where we are.

When I walk into Room 101 in the morning, there are long pieces of paper laid out on the floor. There are designs drawn on each paper, like they're pages from a huge coloring book. I see mushrooms, flowers, trees, grass, and a sky with fluffy clouds.

Lucy, Cara, and I get busy painting.

I start with a big mushroom. Ms. Corazón tells me to make it red and white. She tells Lucy to make her cloud white and make the sky blue. Cara's flower should be pink, with a green stem.

Soon, I have paint on my jeans. I look around and see that lots of kids have paint all over them. I'm glad I didn't wear a fancy dress to school today.

As I'm looking around the room, Paula catches my eye. She stands up, puts her paintbrush down, and starts walking toward me.

I whisper, "Oh no, here comes Paula!"

Paula stands over us and looks down at our pieces of the set. She says, "I see you girls need help. You aren't very creative. I like to do my own designs, and I finished more pieces than anybody."

She points at a few papers on the other side of the room. I can see that she didn't take her time. She made the mushrooms blue. She made the sky green. She made the trees pink.

Normally, I would love pink trees. After all, pink is my color. But that's not how it's supposed to look!

Lucy and I look at each other. I know what she's thinking. We don't need help from someone who thinks the sky is green!

"We're going to follow Ms. Corazón's directions, but thanks anyway," Lucy replies.

Paula frowns. "Suit yourself, if you want ugly, baby drawings," she says.

"It's not babyish to follow directions," Cara says.

"Well, it's babyish to get paint all over yourself," Paula says, pointing at Cara's shirt. There's a splash of green paint on her blue shirt. "I'm the Queen," Paula goes on, looking at me. "And Queens don't get paint on themselves."

I look down at the splatters of paint on my jeans.

Paula stomps away. "Just ignore her," I tell my friends. "She doesn't know the first thing about being a Queen."

We paint all morning. After lunch, we have recess. "Let's play color tag!" Cara shouts.

If you haven't played color tag before, you sure are missing out on the most fun game. One person shouts a color. If you have on that color, nobody can tag you. Since we're all covered in paint, we have on lots of colors.

Paula gets tagged a lot, since she's only wearing blue jeans, red sneakers, and a green shirt. She has no paint colors on her. By the time the game is over, I'm hot from running around so much.

After math we're going to paint some more, so we can be all finished by tomorrow for our final dress rehearsal. That means we will practice the play just like we're really doing it.

We will have our performance on Friday. Momma and Daddy are both going to come. Daddy even took the day off from work!

During math, I see that Paula has a red spot on her forehead. I talk right in Lucy's ear.

I whisper, "Paula has a zit on her forehead just like T.J. gets."

Lucy whispers back, "It's probably paint."

"Nuh-uh. She didn't get any paint on her, remember?" I say.

"What is it, then?" Lucy asks.

I shrug.

By the time painting starts again, I notice three more spots on Paula's face. Plus, she's all sweaty. She keeps scratching her arms and her tummy.

"What's wrong with you?" I whisper.

"Shut up, you big baby," Paula says back. "Leave me alone."

I can't believe she called me a name AND told me to shut up! Rude! But I don't want to tell on her. I think she might be getting sick or something.

I walk over to Ms. Corazón, who is helping Taylor with his White Rabbit costume. She smiles when she sees me. "What's up, Kylie Jean?" she asks.

"I'm getting awful worried about Paula, ma'am," I tell her. "She has spots on her, and it's not paint either."

Ms. Corazón puts down her sewing needle lickety split. She dashes over to Paula.

"Let me look at your face, honey," Ms. Corazón says. Paula sticks her tongue out at me. She knows I'm the one who told Ms. Corazón about her spots.

"I think I better get you down to the nurse," Ms. Corazón tells Paula.

We keep on painting while they're gone, but I keep glancing at the door. I'm worried about Paula.

Even though she's the meanest girl I have ever met in my whole entire life.

When Ms. Corazón comes back, she claps her hands.

"Everyone, please listen up," she says. We all quiet down. "Paula has the chicken pox," she tells us.

Lucy nods. "I had that one time," she says. "I hated it! My mom made me wear socks on my hands so I wouldn't scratch!"

"I'm going to write a note for each of you to bring home," Ms. Corazón tells us.

I raise my hand. "What about the play?" I ask. "Will Paula be better in time for Friday?"

Ms. Corazón sighs. "I don't think so," she says. "I think you'll have to do her part, Kylie Jean, since you're her understudy."

I want to shout and scream with joy, but I don't. Inside, I feel my heart pounding, like I'm scared, but really I'm super happy. I don't want Paula to be sick, but I sure am glad to be Queen!

Chapter Eleven
Not So Mean

When I get home, I tell Momma all about
Paula getting the chicken pox. Momma is glad
that I'm going to be the Queen. But I can't stop
thinking about Paula. Nobody likes her. She won't
even get one visitor. Momma always visits sick
friends and takes them a pot of soup.

"Ugly Brother, do you think I should visit
Paula?" I ask.

He whines and covers his face with his paws.
That means he thinks it's a bad idea, but I already
made up my mind. Paula needs a friend.

I'm too little to make soup, so I pack some cookies and apple juice in my backpack. Then I pack my favorite book, *Ramona the Pest*, too.

Momma is on the phone, so I don't bother to ask her if I can go. I know she'd want me to do nice things for Paula.

"I'm going to a friend's house, but I'll be back for dinner," I shout. I hop on my pink bike with the sparkly streamers and ride to Paula's house. She lives on the same street as Cara.

When I get there, I ring the bell. *Ding-dong.*

Finally, the door opens. It's a lady. I guess it must be Paula's mom. She has a big belly. Not like she ate too many cookies, but like she's going to have a baby.

"Can I help you, honey?" she asks.

"I'm here to see Paula," I tell her. "I'm Kylie Jean. A friend. From school."

The lady smiles. "Oh!" she says. "How nice! But Paula's sick, honey. You don't want to get the chicken pox!"

"Oh," I say. "Well, what if I just go in her room?" I ask. "I won't touch her or anything. I just want to say hi."

Paula's mom thinks for a second.

Finally, she smiles. "I guess that'd be all right," she says. "But only for a second."

"Promise," I say. I cross my heart to show her I mean it.

Paula's mom leads me to Paula's room. "Paula?" she says. "Someone's here to see you." She smiles at me and says, "I'll be back in a minute." Then she walks away.

Paula is lying in her bed, watching TV. Her face is covered with spots. She asks, "What are you doing here, Kylie Jean?"

"I brought you some cookies," I tell her. Then I reach into my backpack and pull out the bag of cookies. She eyes the bag, and I can tell she wants a cookie. I pop one in my mouth. "You want one?" I ask.

Paula nods.

"Okay, but I promised not to touch you, so we'll have to be real quick," I say.

I hold out the cookie. "Grab the other end," I tell her.

Paula reaches for the cookie. Our fingers don't touch when she takes it.

She gobbles up the cookie faster than Ugly Brother can chew up a doggie treat.

I look around.

Her room is painted blue. There's a big easel for coloring, like a real artist would have. Paula has painted a pink mushroom on it. Her Queen of Hearts costume is hanging up on the closet door.

"I like your room," I tell her.

Paula frowns. "Pretty soon I will have to share with the new baby."

"Is your momma having a baby?" I ask.

"Yep," Paula tells me. "It's gonna be a girl." She sighs. "I really wanted a brother. Oh well."

"I have a brother," I tell her. "It's not that great."

"Why'd you come over?" Paula asks.

I shrug. "I don't know," I say. "I thought you'd be lonely. I brought you a book and some juice."

Paula frowns again. "Who's gonna be my part in the play?"

"I am," I tell her.

She looks away for a minute.

Then she says, "Well, I guess you'll be needin' a costume." She points at the Queen of Hearts outfit hanging on the closet door. "You can try on mine."

"Okay," I say. I pull the dress over my head and put on her crown. The dress makes a red puddle at my feet. It is too long, but the cape and the crown both fit. "I bet my momma could sew this to make it shorter," I say. "If it would be okay with you."

For the first time ever, Paula smiles.

"I really wanted to hate you, but I can't," she says. "It was real nice of you to come over to my house. That is the nicest thing that's happened to me since I moved here. So I guess you can make my costume shorter," she tells me. "But you better take it off now. I think my mom will come back soon."

I take off the costume and stuff it into my backpack. Just then, Paula's mom walks back in. "It's time to go, Kylie Jean," she says. "Thanks for coming by."

"Feel better, Paula," I say. "I hope you come back to school soon."

"Thanks for coming over," Paula says. She smiles at me and I wink at her.

As I ride my bike home, I think, *You never can have too many friends.*

Chapter Twelve
Actress Divine

It only takes Momma a minute to sew up the dress so that it fits me. She can sew fast as lightning! I have a pair of shoes that match perfectly. I twirl in front of the mirror in her room.

"You look nice, Kylie Jean," Momma tells me. "I can't wait to see you in the play!"

The next day, I decide I want to wear the costume to school. I put on my gown, shoes, and the cape. I look just like the Queen!

After lunch, when it's time to practice the play, I have to change into my Alice costume. I have to play Alice first. Later I will be the Queen of Hearts.

During the dress rehearsal, even though I'm playing two parts, I don't make one little teeny tiny mistake.

Mr. Peterson, our principal, comes in to watch us. When the play is over, he shakes each of our hands and tells us we did a good job. He shakes my hand and says, "You were a wonderful Queen!"

"She was Alice, too," Cara tells him.

"Wow!" Mr. Peterson says. "That's a lot of lines!"

After school, I get on the bus.

"Mr. Jim, you just have to come see me in the play tomorrow. If you do, I will be happy as a bee in honey!" I exclaim.

Mr. Jim has heard all my lines. I just know he won't want to miss the play.

He nods and smiles when I invite him. "Sure thing, Miss Kylie Jean," he says. "I'll be there tomorrow. I reckon I should see it since a bunch of you kids are going to be in it."

"You should get there extra early, so you can sit in the front row," I tell him. "That way, you can see me wave to you!"

Mr. Jim laughs. "Maybe I will, little lady," he says. "Maybe I will."

I add, "You won't be able to hear Lucy if you sit too far back, but don't tell her, or you might hurt her feelings."

He nods again. "Well, see you then," I tell him. Then I head back to pick out a spot to sit.

Some kids think Mr. Jim is mean. I think he's just fine!

When bedtime comes that night, I roll one way and then the other. Sleep just won't come to me. I try not to think of anything at all, but it's too hard. Imagining sheep, I start counting. Sheep one, with black spots. Sheep two, all white. Sheep three, all black. Sheep four . . .

It takes a long time to count sheep, and I do not even feel one little bit sleepy yet. Sheep don't help you sleep!

Momma checks in on me and sees that I'm still awake. "Are you havin' trouble sleeping, sugar?" she asks.

I nod. "My brain won't turn off!" I tell her.

Momma smiles. "I'll be right back," she promises.

When she comes back in a few minutes, she has my favorite mug, the one with the big pink heart on it. It's full of warm, sweet milk. "Warm milk always helps me sleep when I'm having trouble," she tells me. "Drink it all up. You'll see."

I drink the milk. At first I think it was just a dumb idea like counting the sheep. But then suddenly my eyes feel heavy, and my pink princess bed is so soft.

"Good night, sweetheart," Momma whispers. Then I slip into sleep.

In the morning, I feel great. I get dressed quickly. Then I run downstairs for breakfast. Momma has some super-special pancakes ready for me. They are heart-shaped and have raspberries in them!

Momma says, "Good morning, Queen of Hearts! Today is your big day. You better eat a good breakfast, so you can keep your energy up. We can't have our Queen too tired to say her lines tonight. Right?"

"That's right, Momma," I say.

T.J. comes in. "Guess what, Kylie Jean?" he says.

"What?" I ask.

"Daddy's gonna drive us to school today, since it's your special day," my brother says.

I clap my hands. "Yay!" I say. "That's way better than taking the bus!"

"Yeah," T.J. says. "Mean ol' Mr. Jim won't make your day start off good."

I frown. "Mr. Jim isn't mean," I tell him. "I really like him. He's going to come see my play!"

T.J. looks surprised. "Really?" he asks.

"Yeah," I say. "So don't you go bein' mean about my friend Mr. Jim!"

Chapter Thirteen
In the Spotlight

When I get to school, Lucy and Cara are waiting for me.

"Can you believe it?" Lucy says. "Today is the day! We're doing the play!"

We squeal and hug each other. Then Ms. Corazón says, "Okay, everybody, let's get moving!"

It is crazy in the auditorium. Everyone is rushing around and talking all at once. One girl cries because her makeup makes her look funny. One boy's costume is missing. Finally, we are all dressed and ready.

"Ten minutes till showtime!" Ms. Corazón announces. "Everyone needs to get backstage to wait!"

All of the Alices wait together. I am wearing the dress and wig, because I go first. It is getting very noisy in the theater. Everybody in the whole school is coming in and finding a place to sit.

I peek through the curtain and see about a million kids and parents waiting to see us. Momma, Daddy, Pa, Nanny, Granny, and Pappy are all there to see us.

Cara looks out too. "Wow!" she whispers. "We're going to be famous!"

Mr. Peterson walks onstage. "Ladies and gentlemen, you are in for a treat," he says. "Ms. Corazón's class will now perform *Alice in Wonderland*."

Everyone claps, and I step onto the stage. For just a second, I can't remember my lines. The bright stage lights are blinding me. There are so many people. I open my mouth, and nothing comes out.

Everyone is silent.

Then suddenly I remember what to do. It's just like I'm saying my lines with Ugly Brother, but instead I'm talking to kids in my class. I don't miss a single line.

As soon as I'm done, I rush to change into my Queen costume. Ms. Corazón helps me.

"You look great," she tells me. "You'll do a very good job!"

Then I have to wait backstage until it is time for the Queen of Hearts to go out. I don't worry at all this time. I shout, extra loud, "Off with their heads!" Then I wave at Mr. Jim, sitting in the front row.

Before I know it, Lucy is pretending to wake up and stretch. She says, "I had a very strange dream." Then the lights go off, and the curtain closes.

All of the kids return to the stage. The curtain goes up and lights come on. We take a bow. The room is loud with everyone clapping.

I hear someone shouting, "Bravo!"

Daddy comes to the stage. "Kylie Jean, you will always be my little queen," he says. Then he hands me a bunch of red roses and a little heart-shaped box of candy.

"Thank you, Daddy!" I say. I smell my roses. "These are the prettiest flowers in the whole wide world, and I love you to the moon and back."

I give him a big squeezy hug. People are still clapping, so I run back to the center of the stage and take another bow. My heart is pounding from excitement. I feel like a star!

Chapter Fourteen
More Spots

When I get home from school, Ugly Brother comes right over to me to congratulate me. He licks me on the face.

"You're licking the Queen!" I tell him, laughing.

He barks, "Ruff, ruff."

I head to the bathroom to wash off my special stage makeup. When I look in the mirror, I see a red polka dot on my cheek.

I shout, "Momma, come quick! I have the Chicken Spots now!"

Momma dashes in and takes a good long look at my face. Then she pulls my shirt up to look at my tummy. It's covered with spots. One of them looks like a little red heart.

Momma sighs. "You must have gotten them at school," she says.

"I borrowed Paula's costume," I whisper. "But I didn't touch her! Not even when I gave her a cookie!"

"You will be the Queen of Chicken Pox for the next two weeks," Momma says. "You'll have to stay in bed and drink lots of juice."

"Okay," I say. I don't care. Being sick will give me lots of time to make a plan. Being the Queen of Hearts was really fun, but my real dream is to be a beauty queen!

Recipes from Momma's Kitchen

Momma and I love to cook together. We make all kinds of delicious treats. We like the cooking part, but we like the eating part even more! You and a grown-up can make these recipes together. Yum-o!

The Queen's Sandwich

Makes: 1 sandwich

YOU NEED:

1 four-inch heart-shaped cookie cutter

2 slices of your favorite bread

Your favorite sandwich fillings (peanut butter and jelly, or cheese, or tuna salad, or turkey and lettuce, or whatever you like best!)

Steps

1. Put your favorite fillings onto one slice of the bread. (My favorite is strawberry jelly on whole-wheat bread!)

2. Put the other piece of bread on top.

3. Use the cookie cutter to cut a heart shape out of the middle of the sandwich. (You can throw away the outsides, but I like to eat mine!)

4. Serve and enjoy!

Prize-Winning Blueberry Cream Cheese Pie

Serves: 8

YOU NEED:

1 prepared graham cracker pie crust, chilled

2 cans blueberry pie filling

1 package cream cheese, softened

1/3 cup sugar

1 cup half-and-half or milk

1 package (3 ounces) instant lemon pudding mix

8 oz. container of whipped topping

Steps

1. In a small bowl, mix the cream cheese and sugar until the mixture is soft and well combined. Add the half-and-half or milk and the instant pudding mix. Beat until combined. With a rubber spatula, fold in half of the container of whipped topping.

2. Pour one can of the blueberry pie filling into the chilled pie crust. Then spread the cream cheese mixture on top.

3. Chill for at least four hours.

4. Top with the second can of blueberry pie filling and, if you want, the rest of the whipped topping. Serve immediately.

Red, White, and Blue Jubilee Pops

Makes: 10

YOU NEED:
10 sandwich cookies (the kind with extra filling is the best!)

Red, white, and blue candy melts

Red, white, and blue sprinkles

A package of lollipop sticks

A grown-up helper

Waxed paper

Steps

1. Carefully stick a lollipop stick into the filling of each cookie. Place the pops on a cookie sheet and refrigerate 15 minutes.

2. Ask your grown-up helper to melt the candy melts and put each color in its own glass container. Be careful—this is hot! Line a cookie sheet with waxed paper.

3. Dip each cookie pop into one color. Sprinkle with sprinkles and place on waxed-paper-lined cookie sheet. Move quickly so that the candy doesn't harden too fast. If your candy gets too hard, ask your helper to re-melt it. Cool cookie pops in refrigerator for 10 minutes before serving. Yum, yum!

Marci Bales Peschke was born in Indiana, grew up in Florida, and now lives in Texas with her husband, two children, and a feisty black-and-white cat named Phoebe. She loves reading and watching movies.

When **Tuesday Mourning** was a little girl, she knew she wanted to be an artist when she grew up. Now, she is an illustrator. She especially loves illustrating books for kids and teenagers. When she isn't illustrating, Tuesday loves spending time with her husband, who is an actor, and their children.